VAMPIRE SUN

/ / / /

J.R. RAIN

THE VAMPIRE FOR HIRE SERIES

Moon Dance
Vampire Moon
American Vampire
Moon Child
Christmas Moon
Vampire Dawn
Vampire Games
Moon Island
Moon River
Vampire Sun
Moon Dragon
Moon Shadow
Vampire Fire
Midnight Moon
Moon Angel
Vampire Sire

Published by
Crop Circle Books
212 Third Crater, Moon

Copyright © 2014 by J.R. Rain

All rights reserved.

Printed in the United States of America.

ISBN-13: 978-1548800482
ISBN-10: 1548800481

Dedication

To Sandra again...and again.

VAMPIRE SUN

"We watch you from the shadows, sometimes from within your very homes. We watch you live your mundane, dreary lives...and we wonder why you don't crave more, hunger for more. Live more. But never fear, we shall do it for you. Oh, yes, we will."
—*Diary of the Undead*

1.

I was watching Judge Judy...and wishing I was her.

I didn't wish I was very many people—in fact, very few—but she was one of them. No, I didn't want to be on TV (that was, if I could even show up on TV, which I didn't think I could without copious amounts of makeup), nor did I want to deal with the steady stream of derelicts who filled her courtroom.

I wanted to be confident like her. Fearless like her. Smart like her. Hell, I wanted to *talk* like her, too.

I checked the time on my cell phone. It would probably have been easier to check the time on my watch, had I owned a watch. The last one I'd owned had gotten destroyed on a case. Don't ask. Now, I had my eye out for a shock-resistant, werewolf-resistant and demon-resistant watch. Maybe Timex made one.

My client was late, which I hated. But that gave me more time with Judge Judy, whom I loved. It also gave me more time to finish sewing up Anthony's boxer shorts. These were the third pair of shorts I had mended today. I'd seen enough skid marks to last a lifetime. Hell, this last pair looked like an aerial shot of a drag strip starting gate.

But new boxer shorts cost money, and sewing the old ones was mostly free. And so, like the good mother I was, I powered through Anthony's homage to Jackson Pollack, and sewed the gaping tear in the crotch area. I sewed quickly, deftly, never even poking my finger. The vampire in me heightened all my physical senses, even during the day, but more so at night. Now something as mundane as sewing was almost fun. I still got a kick out of what I could do. I was learning to appreciate who I was, or what I was.

I didn't have much choice, of course.

I either appreciated my current condition or I went mad. I hadn't entirely ruled out the latter. I was only ninety-eight percent sure that I wasn't in a padded cell somewhere, wearing a straitjacket, rocking absently and drooling—looking, on second thought, a lot like Anthony when he played some of his video games.

As I finished sewing the shorts, I heard a car door slam in my driveway. Synchronicity at its best.

I quickly snipped off the thread with my weirdly sharp fingernails—nails that could never, ever be filed down damn them—and hurriedly tossed the shorts in Anthony's room just as the doorbell rang. More good timing, as Judge Judy had just pronounced her latest verdict, a verdict I couldn't have agreed with more.

I smiled, turned off the TV and headed for the door.

I'd like to meet Judge Judy someday.

2.

My client's name was Henry Gleason.

He didn't look like a Henry Gleason. To me, a Henry Gleason should be a big, chubby guy with a cherubic face who gesticulated a lot, and made "to the moon" comments.

This Henry didn't gesticulate. He sat dourly in front of me. His aura was dour, too. Yes, I can see auras. I'm a freak like that. His aura suggested that someone had run over his cat.

"How can I help you, Mr. Gleason?"

I sensed, right off the bat, that there was something drastically wrong. Not even *sort of wrong*, but *chaotically wrong*. His aura was literally spitting fire, snapping around him like solar flares, or so many dragons breathing fire. I kept seeing the image of a small, pleasant-looking woman. These days, I got psychic hits with the best of them. I could also catch fleeting thoughts...words and images. But only those who were tuned into me could catch my own thoughts. This man, this stranger who was about to become anything but a stranger, was not privy to my thoughts. He also wasn't privy to what I was. Or, rather, what I *really* was.

Judging by his mental condition—or lack thereof, as he appeared to have hit some sort of rock bottom—I doubted he would care what I was. Mr. Gleason needed help, and he would have taken it from the devil himself. Little did Henry Gleason know how close he really was to that.

"I need help..." he began, and that was about as far as he got for the next few minutes. He broke down completely, and his aura snapped and flared and shrank in on him. That Henry was a total mess, I had no doubt. Ever the good hostess, I pushed a box of Kleenex his way, although he didn't see it at first.

I waited as he struggled to get hold of himself. I get this sometimes: clients who come into my office and lose it. Generally, it's because a loved one is cheating on them. I don't always take cheating spouse cases. The truth is, I wouldn't take *any* of them if I didn't have to. However, I had something called a mortgage to deal with. And a car note and bills and two kids.

And food...oh God the food. Who knew twelve-year-old girls could eat so much? Anthony I was prepared for. But not Tammy.

Anyway, I mostly took the jobs that came my way. Mostly. Some cases I turned down. Some prospective clients, however, I never heard from again. It sometimes turned out that they just needed a shoulder to cry on. So, the sympathy seekers who came to my home office and cried and got it out of their systems, well, I never saw them again.

You win some, you lose some.

But Henry Gleason wasn't airing his marriage's dirty laundry. He wasn't walking me through, step by step, his wife's sordid affairs or the intricacies of her deception. No, he was weeping for one of two reasons: he was truly hurting, or he was putting on a show.

I would know soon enough which it was. And I was growing more certain it had to do with his wife.

No, I didn't know all. I wasn't God. In fact, I was about as far from God as one could get. But these days I could tell if someone was lying to me. It wasn't very hard for me to learn their secrets. What exactly was going on here, I didn't know. But one thing was becoming obvious: Henry Gleason wasn't putting on a show. His pain was real.

So, I waited. As I waited, I sent him a mental nudge to reach for the box of tissues which, after pausing briefly and cocking his head slightly, he did. He hadn't known I had given him a mental nudge. It was probably better that he didn't.

He blew his nose and gathered himself and said,

"I'm a total and complete mess. I'm sorry."

"I hadn't noticed."

He tried to smile, failed miserably, and gave up. I noted his shaking hands and his darting eyes that never seemed to settle on anything longer than a few seconds, if that.

I decided to kick things off.

"What happened to your wife, Henry?" I asked.

"I-I don't know. How did you know?"

"Never mind that," I said, and gave him another mental nudge to drop it. I asked, "Did you hurt her?"

He looked at me sharply. "No. Never."

His aura briefly flared green. A partial lie. Now I used my demon-given gifts to dip into his thoughts, and slip just inside his aura. Yes, I was cheating a little. Then again, the sun was also stolen from me, along with Oreos and cheesecakes, fettuccine alfredo and mango margaritas. Or mangoritas, which just so happened to be Allison's favorite drink these days. So if the demon inside me —the thing that fueled this supernatural body of mine—could actually give me something back, could actually add value to my life rather than steal from it, then I would take it gladly. *Lord knows enough had been taken from me.*

"Cry me a river, Mom," as Anthony would tell me these days. Kids, they grew up so fast.

Anyway, the ability to read thoughts was a decent trade-off for having to give up dinner at The Cheesecake Factory—not to mention the ability to quickly discern truth from lies was invaluable to my profession. I no longer had to guess if someone was jerking my chain or not.

Now, as I psychically slipped inside his personal space, without him knowing it of course, I dipped into his thoughts, which turned out not to be an entirely good idea. The guy was borderline losing it. No, correction, he *had* lost it. Weeks ago. He'd lost it when his wife had seemingly disappeared at a Starbucks just outside of Orange County, which I had pieced together from his own chaotic memories.

No, not quite chaotic. His mind, I quickly realized, was continuously looping the crime scene. Over and over, even for the few minutes I was inside his head, he relived his last moments with her.

Sit back, I commanded, *relax.*

Henry Gleason looked at me, blinked, and then sat back in my client chair. His thoughts calmed a little and I was able to piece together what I saw. It wasn't a pretty picture.

"Tell me what happened, Henry," I said, and as he spoke, I relived the scene in his thoughts.

***

Henry is waiting impatiently, drumming his fingers on the steering wheel...

His wife has gone inside the Starbucks to grab them some iced mochas. Henry doesn't even like iced mochas. His wife doesn't either. What the fuck is an iced mocha, anyway? And why had she insisted they stop here, dammit? Lucy is acting weird today, he thinks. So weird.

He waits in the heat. His window is down. Hot wind blows through the open window. He checks the time on his cell phone.

I hear him say, "C'mon, babe, where are you?"

More drumming. More hot wind.

He turns around, scans through the back window of a truck toward the busy Starbucks. Nothing. No wife. No damn mochas.

More drumming.

Finally, he gets out and pads across the shimmering asphalt. I can feel the heat. I can also feel the panic rising in him. I know from his thoughts that he has waited about fifteen minutes for her. He thinks she's in the bathroom. Maybe she's sick. If that bitch is in there talking to someone—especially some guy—he was going to go off on her. *Off.* Maybe even slap her around a little. Maybe.

As he heads toward Starbucks, alternately fuming and worried, he tries to remember if she had shown signs of being sick. They had eaten tacos earlier. Yes, the tacos. He is sure of it. They had tasted funny to him.

Now, he's inside the Starbucks. Cool air. People were everywhere. Busy as hell.

He heads immediately to the bathrooms. His mouth literally drops open when he sees a girl exit the bathroom, drops open because it's not his wife.

The girl avoids eye contact with him and hurries past. He glances inside the open door. It's empty. He checks the men's restroom. Empty, too.

I feel his panic. Full-on panic. He dashes out to the lobby, searching, searching. She is nowhere to be found. What the fuck? *What the fuck?*

Now, he's asking employees if they have seen his wife. It's a busy Starbucks. People are coming and going. Workers are making drinks fast, taking orders. Everything is mechanical, rote, all done a hundred times a day, a thousand times a day.

I hear him describe his wife to anyone who will listen. No one remembers seeing her. Wait, one worker does, but she isn't very forthcoming. No, that's not it. She just doesn't remember too much. Yes, she took an order from her. Water only. 'Water?' he asks. 'Are you sure?' 'Yes, sir. Just water. Then she went in there.' She points to the bathrooms.

Henry rushes back to the bathroom. Maybe he missed her. Maybe she is behind the door, or in a stall. Dammit, no stalls. Not behind the damn door. He checks the guys' bathroom again, too. Nothing. Nothing. Nothing.

Now, Henry is outside, rushing back to his truck, in case she has come back, in case he has somehow missed her. But she's not there. Now, he's running around the building, running and running, looking for her. Maybe she had wanted to throw up in an alley? But there's no alley here. Just a big, hot shopping center sitting on the edge of the desert. He stands on a parking lot curb, shielding his eyes from the sun's glare. Nothing. Then stands on his truck's bed, searching.

Nothing.

Now, he's on his cell phone calling the police, weeping, fearing the worst. He's nearly incoherent as he reports her missing.

And then the thoughts repeat.

Over and over.

3.

"She disappeared," said Henry, speaking into his hands, his voice barely audible, his voice barely human. He was unaware that I had just seen the entire scene in his thoughts. "She just disappeared. And I have no idea where she went or what happened."

I didn't know either, of course. I didn't know all or see all. I was just a woman. Just a mom. Granted, a very freaky woman; and, if you asked my kids, I was a very freaky mom, too.

I said, "You watched her walk into Starbucks?"

He nodded. He held a tissue tightly in his hand. The tissue might have been torn to shreds. "Yes. I watched her in the rearview mirror."

I could have confirmed this by dipping into his

thoughts, but I thought I'd had enough of Henry Gleason's thoughts for one day. Hell, for a lifetime. I said, "And you watched her enter?"

"Yes."

"Did you see where she went from there?"

"No. She just, you know, blended with the crowd and I started playing with my phone. You know, wasting time, looking at texts and scores and news and weather."

"*Angry Birds?*"

He gave me a weak grin. "That, too."

"An employee at Starbucks saw her?"

"Yes. She spoke to the police, but she really doesn't remember much."

"Do you have her name?"

"Jasmine."

"Last name?"

He shook his head. "The police will have it, but I can't imagine there are too many Jasmines working at that Starbucks."

I nodded. They would. "Anyone else at Starbucks see your wife?"

"No one."

"What about customers?"

He shook his head. "By the time I went looking for her, anyone who might have seen her was long gone."

"Did you ask around?"

"I did. Like a crazy man. No one had seen her. This isn't your typical Starbucks, you know. People were coming and going, not staying long. There weren't, you know, those hipster geeks in there with their laptops. This Starbucks straddles Corona with Yorba Linda."

I nodded. I knew the area, of course. It was actually a rather great divide, many miles of empty, although beautiful, land, with one lush county segueing into another, harsher, drier, hotter county. The Starbucks wouldn't be your typical hangout for moms and students and guys with square glasses and thick, mangy beards.

No, this Starbucks was a stopover, a place to get coffee while waiting out traffic. Or to use the bathroom. This Starbucks was an outpost. An outlier. Other than the occasional morning commuter who hit up this Starbucks, employees would rarely, if ever, see the same customer twice.

"So, no one else remembered her?"

"No."

"Just the one employee?"

He nodded, said nothing. His aura was crackling with blue energy, split occasionally with streaks of yellow. I wasn't sensing any deception on his part. I felt that I could trust his memory, and I felt that I could trust him, too, although I didn't like the part about him considering hurting her.

"Did you ever hurt your wife?" I asked.

"I told you, she just disappeared—"

"That wasn't my question. Did you ever hit your wife? Hurt her in any way?"

"No, never."

"Did you fight often?"

"What's often? We had your typical fights, I guess."

Despite my desire to stay out of his thoughts, I dipped in quick enough to see him yelling at her—"going off" on her, as he called it. Yeah, he fought like a crazy man. His face twisted. And, no, he didn't hit her. At least, not in the memories I saw. But he was verbally abusive.

"So, what happened next?" I asked, easing back out of his mind again, to my great relief.

"I called the police. Reported her missing."

The police had come out. Had interviewed him and the workers. A massive search had been conducted. The search had lasted for days, and I even remembered it. Whether or not she had been found hadn't made the news. Or, if it had, I was too knee-deep in my own issues to have noticed.

After three days, the search had been called off. There were no leads, nothing to indicate that his wife had ever left the Starbucks. There was video surveillance of her going in, but none of her leaving. A true mystery.

"I didn't kill her, Ms. Moon."

I knew that he didn't kill her. But there was always the slim possibility that his memory had been replaced with a false memory, one so powerful that even his own mind believed it. But I doubted that. Then again, he could have been delusional, of course. Mentally ill. But I doubted that, too. His aura was normal enough. Those with mental health issues had very erratic, scattered auras. Distorted auras that flashed with many colors. His pulsed blue and yellow, and mostly blue. Blue was the color of trust. At least, according to my own experience.

Not to mention, I had seen his memories. Hell, I had lived through them. And then, there was the minor issue that his wife was never seen leaving Starbucks.

"My wife needs help, Ms. Moon. Something has happened to her. Something very, very bad, and the police aren't doing a damn thing about it."

"Nothing?"

"Nothing. The detective on the case, last I heard, was dead."

"Dead? How?"

"I have no clue. They won't tell me anything, other than they're working on it."

"Are you a suspect?"

"They say only that I'm a person of interest. That all husbands are when wives go missing."

True enough. And as I contemplated his words, I checked the time on my cell. Ah, hell. I was going to be late again. *Damn.*

"Will you help me?" he asked.

"Yes. But first, I need to pick up my kids."

4.

Principal West was a middle-aged man with whom I once had a run-in when Danny had told me I was not allowed to pick up our kids from school. Today, the principal gave me the eye, but this time, he did not try to prevent me from picking up my kids.

I waved politely, ducked my head a little, and mouthed, "Sorry I'm late" through the minivan windshield. The principal wasn't happy—and probably made a noise that sounded like *harrumph*, although I could only guess at the noise, since my hearing, although enhanced, wasn't magical.

When I came to a full stop, the principal, who always waited with students for their delinquent parents—I was late far, far too often—finally released my kids to me.

Anthony's jeans might have been hanging down a little in a style that I didn't approve of. Anthony slid into the back seat, and immediately went to work on his Game Boy.

Tammy was sporting a frowning face, in a style I definitely didn't approve of. Since it was her week to sit in the front seat, she rode shotgun.

"I'm almost thirteen, Mom. *Thirteen.* I don't need a principal to wait with me for my mother. It's so embarrassing."

"Your face is embarrassing," said Anthony.

I waved to the principal again, who gave me a tight, half-smile and turned his back on me as I pulled out of the parking lot.

Once we were cruising down Rosecrans, I looked at Anthony in the rearview mirror. "Apologize to your sister," I said to him.

"No."

Aghast, I looked in the mirror again. "What?"

"Just playing. Sheesh, can't you take a joke?"

"No, I can't. Now apologize."

"Fine. Sorry, butthead," he said in Tammy's direction.

"Give me your Game Boy."

He did, passing it to me between the seats. I opened the center console and deposited it within, along with untold work-related receipts, boxes of gum and one mostly covered box of cigarettes. I quickly shut the console again.

"He just called me a butthead, Mom."

"No, I didn't."

"You said it and *thought* it."

"I can think anything I want. There's no law about thinking."

"He just mentally flipped me off, Mom!"

Anthony giggled in the back seat. I told Tammy to get out of her brother's head and for Anthony to quit mentally flipping off his sister. He giggled some more, then settled down. Tammy pouted, crossing her arms, making her own *harrumph* noise. At least they were mostly quiet. It was about all I could ask.

About a minute later, Tammy said, "I saw them, Mom."

"Saw what?"

"The cigarettes. Whose are they?"

It would do no good to give Tammy a line, or tell her anything other than the truth, although I'd rarely made it a habit of lying to my kids. Of course, keeping my vampiric nature hidden from them as long as I could was one thing, but that cat had been out of the bag for some time now. Also, Tammy was as telepathic as I was. Perhaps even more so, since she could read other family members' minds, including her little brother's, and he was about to hit puberty. I prayed for her soul.

"We'll talk about it later," I said.

"What are you two talking about?" asked Anthony. Now that he was no longer physically attached to a game console, he had joined the land of the living.

"Mommy has a pack of cigarettes in the car," said Tammy.

"I want one!" said Anthony, leaning forward between the two seats.

"No, you don't," I said to him, and then glanced at Tammy. "See what you did?"

"I didn't do anything except tell the truth, Mommy."

"Mommy smokes?" said Anthony, perhaps in a higher voice than was necessary. He looked from me to Tammy. "Seriously?"

"I don't know," said Tammy, holding my gaze. "Why don't you ask her?"

I looked at my daughter some more, then over at Anthony's too-eager face, then sighed and pulled the minivan over to the side of the road, where I parked in front of a beautiful, two-story home that was probably even more beautiful inside. My own neighborhood was about two miles away, and was filled with older homes that looked nothing like the ones that lined this street. My small home was the most that Danny and I could afford, and we had been happy to have it. Truth was, I was still happy to have it...but now I associated much pain with it, too. After all, I had been living at that home when my life had been irrevocably changed, when I had gone from being mortal to immortal, when my days were stolen from me, when my husband had rejected me and cheated on me, where my kids had been taken from me, and where I had cried often and still cried to this day. Of course, there were a lot of good memories in that home, too, but with Danny now gone, those memories were getting harder and harder to access.

Perhaps I should have been delighted that Anthony seemed to be coming out of that dark place he had been in for the past few months. In fact, just hearing him playing with his Game Boy was a major step in the right direction. And hadn't he gone many months without teasing his sister? He had, and I had feared that I had lost my kids forever.

But here they were, teasing each other like old times. Yes, I had missed their teasing and fighting and bickering and...

"Don't say it, Mom," said Tammy giggling, and obviously following my train of thought.

"Say what?"

"Farting. You were going to say you even missed Anthony's farting."

"How could I miss his farting?" I asked. "When it never stops."

They both giggled, and I turned in my seat and hugged them both, which was kind of hard to do in the minivan, but we managed. No words were spoken for a few minutes, but we were all soon crying, Anthony the hardest of all. We did this often, now that their father was gone. My tears, however, weren't for Danny. They were for my kids who had lost their father. Danny, in the end, had dug his own grave.

It didn't have to be this way. Danny could have stood by my side, through thick and thin, and through hell and back. We could have stayed a strong family, an unstoppable family.

Such an idiot, I thought, and hugged my kids tighter.

A moment later, Tammy pulled away and said, "Now, about those cigarettes, Mom..."

5.

The anticipated one-hour drive from Fullerton to Corona took four hours, due to a tractor-trailer accident that had blocked several lanes.

Luckily, I had peeled off the freeway before I peeled off any faces. Now, with the sun setting, and me at my jittery worst, I finally sat in the Starbucks parking lot and did my best to calm down, to relax, to breathe.

This was always the worst time of the day for me, the time just before the sun set. It was a time when I felt less than human, when I felt weak and vulnerable.

As I waited, I cracked my neck. I drummed my freakishly long fingernails on the steering wheel. I breathed through my nose, in and out, in and out, rapidly. Faster, faster.

Pacing sometimes helped, but not always. I could get out and pace next to the minivan, but then, I would look like the freak that I am. I stayed inside and waited it out.

Breathing.

Drumming.

Fidgeting.

Last week when I had been pacing, I had inexplicably driven a fist through my bedroom door. I'd regretted that. And it had cost me about a hundred bucks' worth of handyman services.

So, I waited in the minivan, now gripping my steering wheel.

It would do me no good to step out now, not with the sun just minutes from setting. Minutes that felt like forever. Minutes that were truly torture for me.

Now, the setting sun was at the point where I could no longer think or focus on anything else. I just needed to power through the next few minutes.

I breathed and ran my fingers through my hair. I was aware of someone sitting in a nearby car watching me. I didn't want them to watch me. I wanted them to go away. Or I would make them go away.

Breathe, Sam. Breathe. Forget them.

Fuck them.

Breathe, Sam.

And with that last thought, I felt a sudden deep calm overcome me. I didn't have to look up to know the sun had set. My weird, immortal, cursed, supernatural body was hyper-aware of the sun. Attuned to the sun.

I took a deep, full, useless, beautiful breath and felt my lungs expand, and as they expanded, I felt myself expand, too. I felt my energy, strength and vitality noticeably increase.

I went from a shell of a human, to something unstoppable.

Just like that.

I stepped out of the minivan and surveyed the Starbucks where, three weeks earlier, a woman had gone missing.

6.

Unlike some movie vampires, I could go for a few days without eating.

I abhorred the word *feed*. Hell, if anything, what I did was closer to *drinking*. Now, I imagined going an eternity and never really chewing on anything ever again.

It was not my idea of fun, although a brief image of nibbling on Kingsley's fat lower lip did pop into my mind. And I left it there, in my mind. Where it belonged. Hidden and buried.

No, I had nothing against Kingsley. Not even these days. But our time might have come and gone. He had had every chance to be with me, and, in a moment of weakness, had decided that some young floozy was worth more to him than me.

Yeah, it still rankled, and, yeah, I might never truly forgive him for it, even though he had been set up by Ishmael, my one-time guardian angel. Set up to fail.

Still, I happened to believe that his feelings for me should have been stronger than a few minutes with some stranger. But it hadn't been, and to this day, we weren't together because of that.

One strike, I thought, as I stepped into the middle of the mostly empty parking lot, *and you're out.*

Of course, Kingsley had been trying to make up for it ever since, even standing by and mostly keeping his mouth shut as I had dated—and perhaps even loved—another man.

Now that I was single again, Kingsley had respectfully kept his distance, but he'd made it known that he was interested in more. A lot more. That he had gone out of his way, twice, to save me, were feathers in his cap.

We'll see, I thought.

The parking lot was lit with overhanging industrial lamps high up on stanchions, spaced evenly throughout the unusually big lot. Surely, there was more parking here than the Starbucks needed. In fact, I knew this area to be a popular holdover or changeover for people on their way out to, say, Vegas, or down south to San Diego. This was a way station, so to speak, for travelers. Still, why the parking lot was so big was beyond me...until I saw the answer.

And it came in the form of a big, rumbling, diesel smoke-belching recreational vehicle, or RV, pulling into the parking lot from the side road.

As it lumbered toward me, I saw immediately the benefit of the epic space, to accommodate the bigger vacation vehicles, and, undoubtedly, big rigs, too.

Yes, it was a true way station.

The RV parked in due course. A moment later, an elderly couple stepped out, stretched, and headed up to Starbucks. Both smiled and said hello to me. I smiled, too, and turned and watched them go.

That I briefly envisioned pinning them down and feasting, first off the man and then off the woman, should have caused me more alarm than it did.

In fact, the thought seemed perfectly normal.

Uh, oh.

Snap out of it, kiddo, I thought, and heard Kingsley's voice in my head. Or was it Fang's? Maybe a blending of the two.

I focused on the task ahead. The task being, of course, to figure out how a grown woman had disappeared off the face of the earth inside of a Starbucks.

Standing in the center of the parking lot, I turned in a small circle as the sky above grew darker. As it grew darker, the tiny filaments of light that only I could see, appeared, slashing and darting and giving depth and structure to the night. A million fireflies. Hell, tens of millions. Billions. All flashing and forming and reforming.

Early on, the flashing lights had nearly given me seizures. They had taken some getting used to. Now, I knew that each particle of light was, in fact, giving life to the night itself. They formed a sort of staticy laser light show for me and me alone. Now, seeing them was second nature for me. Up close, there was less static. What these light particles were, I didn't know, but I always suspected I was seeing the hidden energy that connected all of us. Humans and vampires alike.

Spirits themselves seemed to be composed of this very energy, as I had watched countless such entities form and reform, disappear and reappear, all using this sort of Universal Energy.

Weird shit, for sure, but welcome to my life.

Now, I searched within the staticy light particles for something that could be dead. Something that could be watching me in return. But I saw nothing. Just the dancing lights that jived and boogied through my vision.

The lack of spiritual activity was significant. It meant that someone *hadn't* recently passed here. That someone hadn't, in fact, been murdered. This, of course, was just conjecture on my part and was based on my own personal experience with the spirit world. Murdered souls often lingered, sometimes for decades, in the locations of their deaths. I had seen such souls. Hell, I had seen a few today when I was driving along the freeway, standing by the side of the crowded thoroughfare, and forlornly watching the living drive by. These, I knew, had perished there on the freeway, in car accidents, no doubt.

Why the dead lingered, I didn't know, but I had seen my fair share of them. So much so that they were now part of my life. My creepy, creepy life. In my experience, spirits appeared in one of three ways: either as souls visiting the living, as the forgotten dead, lost and haunted, or as a *memory* of itself, neither alive nor dead, repeating itself over and over.

I saw none of that here.

Murder sites also had an effect on the environment. A very obvious effect. At such a location, the swirling light energy was even more chaotic. It would swirl and scatter and explode...reminiscent of an active volcano spewing magma. Often, though, I would see another kind of energy within this disturbance. Spirit energy, too. The murdered victim, in fact. Not always, but often.

There was no such energy here. Instead, the light particles swept through naturally, peacefully, unhindered by the shock of death.

I walked the perimeter of the expansive parking lot, which took a few minutes. The east side consisted of a low shrub wall that bordered the Taco Bell next door. At this hour, Taco Bell had more customers than Starbucks, with a line of cars wending through its drive-thru. I spied surveillance cameras above and around Taco Bell. Anyone heading this way would have been picked up by the

Bell's cameras, too. I logged this away for future inquiry.

I continued around the perimeter. The south-facing part of the lot, opposite the driveway into the parking lot, was interesting. There were lots of places where someone could hide here. A strip of land bordered it, with the freeway itself next to it. Trash and weeds crowded for space, all of which I saw clearly, thanks to the bright streaks of light that illuminated the night. I continued standing there, scanning.

Sure, there were lots of places to escape to, once a person actually left the Starbucks cafe. So far, there was no evidence of Lucy Gleason ever leaving, only entering.

I studied the Starbucks from the parking lot, taking it in. It was part of a small strip mall: attached to it was a dry cleaner, and next to that was a Subway. The Taco Bell was in the next parking lot over, separated by a shrub wall.

I spotted two surveillance cameras, one on each side of the building. Starbucks itself had only one entrance inside, with a rear entrance as well. I frowned and studied the scene, biting my lower lip, but not hard enough to draw blood.

Next, I went inside the Starbucks. It was a typical 'Bucks, as Tammy would call it. She was the coffee addict in the family. I was a very different kind of addict. This 'Bucks had all the sleek, postmodern, industrial décor that one came to expect from a Starbucks. A lot of seating. Open space, with a small hallway that led off to the bathrooms. I examined the women's. Typical: a single room with the toilet in the far corner. A sink. A metal trash can. Nowhere to hide. A quick peek in the men's restroom suggested the same.

I sighed, and then headed out to the lobby. I ordered a venti water, which sounded a lot fancier than it looked. I sat in the far booth and studied the interior, searching for any psychic hits or evidence of foul play.

I got neither.

I hate when that happens.

7.

The three of us were jogging.

A human, a vampire, and a witch. Yes, I know it sounds like the opening to a bad joke: a human, a vampire, and a witch go to a bar. The human orders a glass of wine. The vampire orders a goblet of blood. The witch orders a magic potion. Or something like that.

"Well?" asked Allison.

"Well, what?"

"What's the punchline?"

"I don't know," I said. "I was making it up as I go."

"Oh, God," said Mary Lou, "are you two doing your mind-thingy again?"

"That might be the first time I heard anyone call

telepathy a *thingy*," said Allison. For the most part, Allison and my sister, Mary Lou, got along marvelously.

Except...

Except Mary Lou, as the only one of us without any obvious extrasensory abilities, felt like the odd woman out. I suspected she might be a little jealous of my friendship and easy communication with Allison. I reminded my sister that, as of yet, I had no ability to read her mind, which was the case for all of my blood relatives. It was no slight on her, and it didn't mean I loved her any less. My daughter, of course, was a different story; she could read family members' minds, mine included.

Your daughter, thought Allison, telepathically following my train of thought, *is going to be powerful.*

I'm not sure what to think about that, I thought back.

But it's not going to happen for a while still, came Allison's reply.

Oh? Is that a psychic hit? I silently asked my friend, whose own psychic abilities were getting scarily strong.

Scary?

Scary as in unknown.

Nice catch, thought Allison. *And, yes, that is a psychic hit. I do, after all, work for a prestigious Psychic Hotline.*

I grinned. In fact, Allison was one of the few legit psychics who worked at the Hotline, as she called it. Recently, her cases had become... interesting, to say the least.

Only if you consider removing a demon from the world's most haunted house as interesting, she thought.

Oh, I do, I thought. *And you can quit bragging.*

Yes, my friend was growing more and more powerful. And apparently, her head was growing bigger, too.

I heard that, she shot back. *And it's not. I still have nightmares about that night.*

As she thought those words, I saw the image that flashed through her mind, the image of a man killing himself before her, a man who had been demon-possessed himself.

I should have shuddered at watching the image of the knife being drawn across the man's own throat. I should have been horrified by the blood that spilled down like a crimson waterfall. I should have been shocked, revolted and scared. But I was none of that.

I was intrigued.

I was interested.

I was...excited.

You scare me sometimes, Sam, came Allison's words. *I mean, really scare me sometimes.*

I scare myself, too.

"Oh my God," said Mary Lou. "You two are so rude. I'm right here, you know."

"We're not talking about you, Mary Lou," I said.

"Well, then, how about talk *to me*? As in, include me in your conversation. It's seriously rude to *think* behind someone's back. Or whatever. You know what I mean!"

I looked at Allison and she looked at me and we both snorted.

"It's not funny, you guys," said Mary Lou, slowing down. As she slowed down, her massively heaving chest slowed down, too. And so did the bouncing eyeballs of any and all guys that we passed. "It's rude to us immortals."

"Mortals," I corrected, and did all I could to stifle a giggle. I heard Allison giggling in my head. "I'm *immortal*. You're *mortal*."

"Well, whatever. You're still my sister and you're still being rude."

"You're right," I said. "I'm sorry."

"I mean, I've gone through just as much shit as you guys. Maybe more so. I think I deserve, at this point, to be let in on all your secrets."

"*Some* of our secrets," I said. "Trust me, there are some things you don't want to know."

"Well, let me be the judge of that."

I shook my head as we continued to jog. Yes, Mary Lou had had a rough time a few months ago, of that there was no doubt. She'd been kidnapped by Rachel Hanner, a homicidal vampire who happened to be a Fullerton PD homicide cop—a vampire who had been my one-time friend. Although Mary Lou had been threatened, and Fang had held a knife to her throat, she hadn't been hurt.

Still, I could only imagine her fear when she'd been attacked and taken hostage. Yes, it had been a bad day for my sister. But that didn't mean she should know every deep, dark secret that I had.

"We'll see," I said, and left it at that.

My sister didn't like that answer, but mercifully, let it go.

Although the sun had set an hour ago, the western sky was still aglow with oranges and yellows and reds. I loved that glow. It meant the damnable sun had finally moved on. It meant the worst part of my day—the part just before the sunset—was finally over. It meant I could relax. It meant I could be all that I'm capable of being. It meant I could be who I was meant to be.

A killer.

I shook my head as we jogged. Those words, of course, were not mine. They were *hers*. The demon that possessed me, although *demon* wasn't quite the right word. She had been human once, mortal once. But now, she was so much more.

A highly evolved dark master.

A fancy title, I thought, for a murderous bitch.

Her words appeared in my mind only rarely. But when they did, I always got a jolt, followed by a cold chill. And, trust me, it was damned hard to give a vampire a cold chill. Anyway, I was certain I would never get used to her words in my head.

In fact, I *never* wanted to get used to her words. Hell, I was doing all that I could to eradicate her from my life, forever.

I get the heebie-jeebies, too, Sam, came Allison's own distinct voice in my head. A softer voice, and maybe a little nasal.

Nasal? Now that's just rude.

But true, I thought.

Whatever.

Mary Lou stopped running, although her chest didn't get the memo. It jiggled and settled for a few long seconds afterward. "You two are doing it again." My sister might have sounded exasperated.

You are entirely too focused on your sister's chest, thought Allison.

Quiet, I hissed mentally, *I think we're in trouble. And I'm not focused on her chest. It's just, well, so big. How can you not focus on it?*

"Unbelievable! The two of you are actually *still* doing it while I'm standing here pissed. I'm going home."

"Wait, Mary Lou," I said, grabbing her shoulder. She had turned off the boardwalk and was about to cross some random parking lot. We were at least a mile or so from where our cars were parked. "I'm sorry. Really, I am. Telepathy is just, well, easy. And this one—" I jabbed a finger at Allison "—always seems to be *in* my mind."

"Well, you're always in *my* mind."

I ignored her, although we both knew that wasn't true.

Speak for yourself, she thought.

"Unbelievable," said Mary Lou. "Please tell me you aren't *still* doing it. Please tell me you wouldn't keep disrespecting me like that."

She was about to storm off when I caught her elbow. She yanked her arm free—or tried to—and only succeeded in hurting herself. She yelped and I released her. She now stormed down the boardwalk. At least she was going in the right direction. Allison and I watched her go.

"Well," I said, "what a fine mess you got me into."

"She'll be okay," said Allison.

I sighed. My sister could hold a grudge with the best of them...and she was only now coming out of her shell over the traumatic events of a few months ago. No, she hadn't seen my husband get killed, hadn't watched the dagger plunge into his chest, as I had. But she had *heard* him die. She had *heard* him scream out...and she had heard his ragged breathing as the blood from the wound had filled his lungs.

Yeah, she had been traumatized, perhaps even for life. I took in a big lungful of worthless air and watched her go, walking as fast as she could away from me.

I sighed again and grabbed Allison. "Let's catch up to her."

8.

I was alone in my garage.

Not too long ago, I had broken up with my last boyfriend in this very garage. That something like me could even have something so normal as a "boyfriend" was almost laughable. But I had tried. And I had tried with a mortal, someone who wasn't a bloodsucker.

I swiped open a packet of cow and pig blood with a fingernail that was too long and too sharp to be normal. Concealing my hands was one of the many drags in my life. Drinking from these filthy packets was another.

Yes, a few months ago, my relationship had come to an end when I had finally realized that my boyfriend, Russell, was, in fact, a *love slave*. No, not a sex slave. There's a difference. He was devoted to me unerringly, irrationally, supernaturally. I didn't so much as break up with him as *release* him.

Instantly, the strong, coppery, putrid smell of nearly rancid animal blood wafted up from the open packet. Mercifully, the butchery had delivered a cleaner-than-usual batch of blood, with the last few packets being nearly contaminant-free. In fact, I had almost—almost—enjoyed the packets.

Okay, that might be pushing it. But at least I hadn't gagged.

I wasn't so lucky with this bag. As I looked at the opaque bag, now swollen with blood—like a fat, wingless mosquito—I saw the hair and flotsam. Bits of bone and dirt and muscle and sinew—whatever had been collected as the pigs and cows bled out.

As I watched the particles drift within the bag, I realized something disconcerting. There were, if anything, even *more* particles. Perhaps the other bags had been cleaner, but I doubted it. I had assumed they were cleaner because I hadn't gagged, because I had, in fact, quite enjoyed the bag of filth. No, not as much as I enjoyed drinking from Allison. Drinking from her was...heavenly.

But the past two bags had been quite...tasty.

Uh oh, I thought.

Now, as I raised it before me, careful not to spill the precious contents and watched the constellation of filth rotate slowly, I knew I was in trouble.

Real trouble.

But I didn't care. This was blood, after all. Precious blood.

Delicious blood.

Not as delicious as Allison, but it was good enough.

"Good enough," I whispered, and a small part of me tried to rebel when I licked my lips. "Yes, good enough."

Now, with my children doing homework in the house adjacent to the garage—and, no doubt, sneaking in time on the Xbox One—I tilted the bag of filth to my lips...and drained every last drop. I even tore open the bag and licked it clean.

Lord help me.

9.

You there, Fang?

It was the same question I asked night after night, for the past three weeks, logging on to my old AIM instant message account. The same account Fang and I had first connected through. The account where I had told a complete stranger all of my secrets. Secrets he had used to eventually find me.

I often wondered if I had *wanted* Fang to find me. If I had, in fact, *purposely* dropped enough clues for him to eventually locate me in my small part of the world.

Fang, at the time, had been my only connection to the supernatural. Although not supernatural himself at that time, he had been my source of all things vampiric. His knowledge had been deep and accurate and I missed our easy word play and mild flirtation. In short, I missed my confidant.

Sometimes, I wanted to believe that he had been stolen from me, but I knew that wasn't the case. He got exactly what he had always wanted: *immortality*. He had simply taken matters into his own hands...and had joined the wrong team.

But what was done was done. Fang had gotten his wish, and a whole lot of people were dead because of it. No, my ex-husband's murder wasn't a direct result, but the turning of Fang had caused a domino effect that was still reverberating in my life to this day.

And, yeah, there was the small matter of those joggers Fang had killed. Those and surely others. Perhaps many others.

I couldn't think about that.

Suddenly depressed, I sat back in my office chair and looked at my cell phone. No texts. No missed calls. Not even a Facebook update. The world was asleep at this hour. The mortal world. My kids were sound asleep. Although Anthony was showing some disturbing vampiric tendencies, one of them, thankfully, was not sleeping during the day.

Thank God.

Sure, I had plenty of work to do. These were, after all, my working hours. I knew that most freaks like me were out partying or hunting or running through graveyards, or whatever the hell it was that vampires did together. I had a car payment due next week, not to mention the taxes on the house were due in two weeks. I didn't have time to run through graveyards. I had to make some money.

I looked at the stack of printouts next to my computer. One of my jobs was to run background checks for various companies. I had, for instance, a deal with the Hyundai dealership down the road. When they got new prospects, they provided me with their job applications, and I checked out their criminal histories.

A stack of names. With addresses, including social security numbers, phone numbers, and all their pertinent contact info. With a little digging, I could find out if, say, they lived alone. A Google Maps search would let me know if, say, they had neighbors nearby or far away, neighbors who might hear them scream, or not.

I drummed my long nails on the stack of prospects, most of whom were probably waiting anxiously to hear if they got the job or not. Not one suspected that an honest-to-God vampire was looking a little deeper into their private lives.

I wondered how they would feel about that.

Would they be nervous? Or scared?

I suspected both. I also suspected they didn't believe in vampires. But they would believe, oh, yes, if I showed up on their doorsteps. Then they would be very, very nervous. No, frightened.

Terrified.

Yesss, good.

I knew *she* was speaking to me. The devil bitch

that lived inside me. She had been gaining some ground in my mind. What that meant, exactly, I didn't know.

But I felt it.

And, for tonight, I didn't care.

Instead, I thought again of the new hires. The thought of anyone fearing me intrigued me. No, not quite *intrigued* me. *Excited me.*

I swallowed, licked my lips.

I felt my heartbeat pick up a little. It went from beating maybe five times a minute to twenty or thirty. *Yeah, I'm a freak through and through.*

No, Sssamantha. You are a hunter.

Yes, I thought. *A hunter.*

I liked that. I would be a damn good one, too. No, I'd never hunted a living person for the express purpose of killing them, just for killing's sake. Other vampires did this. Not me. Indeed, other vampires explored their true natures.

Not me, though.

Not until now. I needed to do something about that. I needed to hunt the living, to feel their fear, to taste their blood, and to live again. To really, truly live.

I knew it was the demon bitch inside me, encouraging me, influencing me, possessing me...but I didn't care.

Not true, I thought suddenly, shaking my head. *I do care. I care very much.*

Alarmed, I sat up. I had to care. *I had to.* Caring was the only thing that separated me from her. And the demon was a *her*, too. I sensed her repressed femininity. I sensed that she had been enamored with her own good looks, too. She had been beautiful once, I felt. Interestingly, I sensed she might have been a mother once, too, but I could be wrong. Either way, more and more of her was creeping through, bubbling up from the depths. Whether or not she controlled what came through to me, I didn't know. Perhaps the information that came through was random. Perhaps not. Perhaps the information was carefully provided, controlled, designed to do exactly what it was doing to me right now: *breaking me down.*

No, I thought. *No, dammit. No one is breaking me down.*

The bitch inside me didn't often express herself clearly by using complete sentences or stringing together a coherent thought. I suspected she couldn't. I suspected our connection wasn't complete, and so, only parts of her came through. Random, stray thoughts.

More often than not, she came through via feelings. At first, I had always known it was her. At first, her bloodlust thoughts were easily distinguishable from my own. Now, not so much.

Now, her thoughts felt natural, comfortable. Even worse, they felt like my *own* thoughts. This should have scared me. In the least, it should have worried me. But it didn't, not anymore.

She was a powerful entity. I would benefit from her presence in my life. She would benefit, too. She would live again, and I would have untold strength.

"Now, dammit, get the fuck out of my head."

I stood, pacing, fighting her presence, recalling how the entity within Hanner had possessed her completely. Would that happen to me? What would it feel like to have another control my body? To speak for me? To act for me? To think for me?

I paced in the small space behind my desk, careful of power cords. Why I had so many power cords, I didn't know. I spotted a charger for my phone, my iPad, my Kindle and even one for a Nook. I didn't even own a Nook.

I avoided it, along with myriad of other cords that seemed to multiply behind my desk, all of which served some damned purpose.

Except the cords weren't what was really troubling. No, my mind was on *possession*. On, in fact, *losing* my mind. Of having it being stolen by another.

"No!" I said, pacing faster and faster. Now, my foot did get caught in the Nook cord. I kicked it, and it came out. Along with all the other wires in the wall.

Cursing—but thankful I had something to distract me—I went about plugging all the wires back in, praying I got them right. A moment later, when I had successfully turned on my computer again, there was Fang's response, waiting for me in the AOL message chatroom.

Hi, Moon Dance.

10.

We hadn't spoken in many months, not since Fang had shown up one night, here in my office, when he revealed to me that he had killed many.

Fang had been, of course, compelled to kill by a very old vampire, a vampire who was now dead, thanks to Kingsley. With the old vampire's death, the connection had been severed and Fang had come instantly to my rescue, and for that I would be forever thankful to him. That he had killed many while *not* compelled was cause for much concern.

Now, of course, I was having a hard time remembering why the killing of innocent people had bothered me so much. After all, wasn't killing in a vampire's nature? Yes, it was. To kill and to feed and to grow stronger and stronger...

Yesss. Good, Sam, good.

I shook my head and ran my fingers through my thick hair. It was her, of course.

"Not me," I said, gasping a little. "Go back to hell."

I took a few deep, steadying breaths and looked again at the words on the laptop screen before me, framed around the AOL chat window.

Hi, Moon Dance.

I raised my fingers to the keyboard, and began typing...

***

Hi, Fang.

He didn't immediately reply. I waited a few minutes, my clawed fingers hovering over the keyboard. The image of a gargoyle perched on the ledge of an old building came to mind. For some reason, I smiled.

No, *she* smiled. She liked dark things, disturbing things. Granted, gargoyles were hardly the things of nightmares. No, she was pleased that her thoughts were so quickly coming to the surface. That her thoughts were mingling easily with my own.

I shook my head again, fought off a brief wave of panic, and typed: *You there, Fang?*

A minute passed. My house was so quiet that I could literally hear my kids' heartbeats. Anthony's beat a little slower than Tammy's. Was that because of the vampire blood in him? My heartbeat rate was only a fraction of that of a human's. Had I committed my son to a lifetime of making excuses for who he was, and why he was different? Maybe. But the alternative was far, far worse. Better a lifetime of excuses than no life at all.

Not too long ago, the thing within had tried to escape using another means: procuring all four magical medallions, medallions meant to help vampires battle that which lives within them. At least, that was what the alchemist Librarian had told me, and Archibald Maximus should know, since he had created the medallions in the first place. Like all things in life, there was a loophole, a way for something good to be used for something bad. Turns out, the collecting of all four medallions at once could also release the demons within. On a desolate island in the Pacific Northwest, I had been lured to my destruction. That hadn't quite happened, and my son, who had actually *consumed* one of the medallions in a liquefied form, could live on.

And live on he did, growing faster than other boys his age, stronger than other boys his age, and, if you asked me and his older sister, gassier than other boys his age.

I almost smiled. The thing within me didn't want me to smile. It didn't like innocent jokes. It didn't like humor.

"Well, fuck you," I said, and smiled anyway.

And that was when the AOL chatbox flickered and the status read: "Fang950 is typing."

***

Hello, Moon Dance.

Fang and I used to have a strong telepathic link. So strong that we could often hear each other's thoughts over a great distance. Now, since becoming a fellow creature of the night, that link was broken. He was inaccessible to me, and that was a loss greater to me than I was willing to admit.

You are up late, Fang, I typed.

Or early, he wrote back almost immediately.

I smiled, pleased to see some of his old personality coming through. My last memory of Fang had been troubling at best. He was robotic, lifeless, and, if you asked me, lost.

Now that I had him, I wasn't sure what to say to him. It had been many months since we had last spoken, and many more before that when our relationship was irrevocably changed. After some false starts, I finally wrote: *Still a vampire?*

Or something.

I nodded to myself. Yes, being a vampire wasn't all it was cracked up to be. A *host* was more accurate.

Where you living now?

In L.A.'s Echo Park district.

Still bartending?

I almost, *almost* sensed him laughing, but probably not. He would have laughed at that, but not anymore.

No, Moon Dance.

Okay, I'll bite. No pun intended. What are you doing for work these days?

I don't need to work, Sam.

I nodded to myself, suddenly getting it. *Hanner left you money. Probably a lot of money.*

Something like that.

Of course, Hanner wouldn't have had a traditional will, not when she was over a century old. Besides, whoever heard of a vampire having a will? More than likely, Hanner had simply given Fang access to her accumulated wealth. Probably the case with other vampires, with money being passed to each new generation of bloodsuckers. I was probably the only idiot vampire who actually worked. For all I knew, Fang was sitting on top of a pile of gold, stolen and stockpiled by the ageless and undead. No doubt stolen and looted from countless victims. Or, even better, just given to them by compelled victims.

I could do something similar, I knew. I could, with some training, stand outside the local Bank of America, and compel all those who came and went to empty their savings accounts for me. In fact, it would probably be easy to do.

Indeed, the entity within me perked up at this line of thinking. Yes, she and her kind were used to living this way, of manipulating and exploiting and destroying.

I pushed her out of my mind, or as far out as I could.

So, you do nothing, then? I asked him. *Just*

sitting around and drinking goblets of blood?

Oh, there is much I do, Sam. Some things I can talk about, some I can't.

You are setting up another blood bank, I wrote. No, I might not be able to read his mind anymore, but I was also a trained investigator who happened to be pretty good at her job.

Yes, Sam, but it's not what you think.

And what am I thinking?

That we are killing people, draining them dry, like Robert Mason did in Fullerton.

And Hanner, I said. *Let's not forget her role.*

Indeed, her role had been to help the murders slip through the cracks, to help the police forget, to hide and manipulate the facts.

Fang was writing something, and then paused. I knew this because the words "Fang950 is typing" had been flashing in the upper corner and then it quit flashing. I really didn't know what he was going to write, but a part of me thought he might have been about to defend Hanner.

He loved her, I suddenly thought. *He loved her and he'd killed her...*

Killed her for me.

I knew that Hanner and Fang had been close. I knew that she had taught him the ins and outs of vampirism, something that had never been taught to me. Hell, it still seemed I was learning something new every day.

Yeah, it stood to reason that the very creature who had turned him, trained him, and fed him in his early days would be the object of his affection.

I got it. I understood it. I was sure it would have happened to anyone.

But that didn't stop me from feeling jealous.

And yeah, I got all of this from a simple hesitation, a simple pregnant pause. It might as well have been pregnant with twins.

Whatever that meant.

Anyway, after his telling hesitation, he started writing again. *The Hanner operation was flawed,* he wrote. *Most of the victims didn't have to die.*

Most? I wrote. *Wouldn't it be more human to say that "none of them needed to die"?*

Yes, of course. I was loose with my speech. Or with my fingertips.

I nearly asked what else he was loose with. It was a damn good thing Fang couldn't read my mind.

Then again, why was I feeling jealous? Fang had, after all, practically thrown himself at me. But our timing had never been right. And then, the dumbass had to get himself turned into a fellow creature of the night. Yes, but the Fang I had developed feelings for wasn't the same Fang I was corresponding with now. At least, I didn't think it was. Who this new Fang was, well, I would just have to wait and see.

So, how are you running things differently? I asked, typing.

It's an underground blood bank. We pay the humans for their blood.

How do you recruit them?

Someone who knows someone. Word gets around in the right places.

Addicts, I wrote. It wasn't a question.

Drugs don't affect our system, Sam. You should know that. And if you didn't, you do now.

I could almost—almost—hear Fang's enthusiasm. Yes, he was finally a creature of the night. The thing he had wanted most in the world. More than even me.

You're recruiting crackheads, I typed.

Not all are addicts, Sam. Some are normal people, everyday people. They give us blood and go home. There's no reason to kill anyone and draw attention to ourselves.

Are you doing it for the money?

No, Sam. I don't need money. Not anymore. But others who are working for us—the humans—yes, they are very much doing it for the money.

You're working with crooks?

In a word, yes.

And this is why I haven't heard from you? I wrote. *Because you were putting together this...operation?*

There was a long pause, and then this: *I had my reasons for being away, Sam. Yes, I was putting together this operation, but mostly...*

He stopped there, so I finished for him: *Mostly, you were mourning her.*

Yes, Sam.

You loved her.

In a way, yes.

More than me?

Not now, Sam. I'm not ready to talk about any of this now. Please.

Fine. Sorry. I collected myself, took in a deep breath and wrote: *So, how, exactly, does this operation work?*

We're more efficient now, he wrote. *And we have a consistent, steady supply of blood.*

Are all of your "suppliers" willing suppliers? I asked.

I'm not going to lie to you, Sam. Not to you, not ever. Some of our sources will never know what happened to them.

These would be your fresh sources?

Yes, Sam, he typed. *Those who provide blood straight from the vein, if you will.*

Where do you find these sources?

Same place, he typed. *They are simply led to a special room...*

Where a vampire is waiting.

Yes.

Who feasts from the victim, and then compels them to forget.

Yes, but those are only rare occasions. Mostly, we collect blood in these facilities. It's win-win, Sam. No bodies, people get paid. Everyone is happy.

I should have been repulsed, disgusted, alarmed, or at least concerned. I was none of these things. I was, if anything, greatly intrigued. And I didn't even think it was *her* who was intrigued. No, the person I was now, the thing I had become, saw the useful practicality in Fang's enterprise.

And, I reasoned, was my arrangement with Allison much different? She permitted me to drink from her, not for monetary gain, but for extra-sensory gain. To increase her sixth sense. We, in effect, used each other. If there was ever a codependent relationship, this was it.

Yes, for vampires to exist, we needed blood. But we didn't need to kill and draw attention to ourselves. Fang had figured out an efficient enterprise. I admired him for it.

Lord help me, I *admired* him.

I have to go now, Sam.

Okay, I wrote. *Talk later?*

Of course. Goodnight, Moon Dance.

Goodnight, Fang.

And with that, he signed out.

11.

I was back in the City of Corona.

This time, I was at the Corona Police Department. The city, which boasted more than a hundred and fifty thousand people, also had, unfortunately, a thriving homicide department.

Detective Jason Sharp was exactly that: *sharp*. Or, more exact, *angular*. His young face segued into a pointy chin. His cheekbones were to die for. At least, for a woman. His nose was long and arrow-like. He looked a bit like a drawing come to life. He wore a white, long-sleeved shirt buttoned snugly at his throat. His Adam's apple rested directly on top of his collar. It bounced and bobbed seemingly with a will of its own. Next to his Adam's apple was a thick, carotid vein. It pulsed every now and then. But that might have been my imagination.

Detective Sharp was busy bringing up a file on his computer screen. I couldn't see his computer screen, although I could see it glowing in his eyes—eyes that flashed and darted in their sockets like butterflies on crack. If I had to guess, I would say Detective Sharp had some serious A.D.D. going on. My son's eyes darted around like that, scanning everything, seeing everything, absorbing everything, reading everything. I always suspected my son had A.D.D. My son was a gamer. I wondered if Detective Sharp was a closet gamer, too.

I said, "You're new to the case."

"Yes."

"Who was the original detective?"

"Renaldo," he said.

"And where's Renaldo?"

"Parkview Cemetery."

"Dead?"

"Gee," he said, glancing at me. "You must be a real detective."

"I was an agent, too," I said.

"Federal?"

"Yup," I said.

"Sorry if I sounded like an ass."

"Oh, you did."

"It's just that some blowhard private dicks come in here with all sorts of swagger—and don't know shit about what they're talking about. I didn't know you worked for the feds."

"Now you do."

"Now you're on your own?"

"I am."

"Happy?"

"Turns out I like working for myself. I happen to be a helluva boss."

He laughed. "I couldn't do it. I need someone riding my ass all day. Otherwise..."

"Otherwise, you would play HALO all day."

"You sound like you're judging me."

"My son plays HALO," I said.

"It's a good game—"

"My son is ten."

"These are more than just games, they're experiences."

"If you say so," I said. "How did the previous detective die, if you don't mind me asking?"

"A car accident."

"I'm sorry to hear that."

"So am I. He was a good guy. We miss him here."

"When was the accident?"

Detective Sharp shrugged. "Three weeks ago."

I made sympathetic sounds that I didn't really feel. Truth was, these days, I found death a lot less... heartbreaking. I found death. More...interesting. Exciting, even.

No, *she* found death exciting.

Deep breaths, Sam.

"Can you tell me any more than that?" I asked.

He studied me, then nodded. "Broadsided over on Grand Street and Main."

"Broadsided by who?" I asked. And just as the word escaped me, I silently cursed myself, certain it should have been "by whom." Sigh. I might be undead, but that didn't make me a grammarian.

"We don't know."

"Hit and run?"

"Yeah."

"You knew him well?"

"Well enough."

"Any leads?"

"We got some."

"But nothing you're willing to pass along?"

He studied me some more, then shook his head. "No," he said. "Not until I know you better."

"I could help."

"We got enough help."

"Fine," I said. "What do we know about Lucy Gleason?"

"The broad who went missing from Starbucks?"

"Yeah."

"We know she's still missing."

"What else?"

He studied me some more. He wasn't sure if he liked me, which was hard to believe. He already felt like he'd said too much, which wasn't much at all. I knew all of this because I was following his thoughts. He was just about to turn me away, claiming he was busy—he was, but not *that* busy—when I gave him a gentle telepathic nudge, planting the words directly into his mind:

Tell her everything. And get her a glass of water.

He blinked, nodded, and then said, "Follow me. And would you like some water?"

"Why, how kind of you, Detective," I said and followed him out, hiding a grin. I should have felt bad that I was controlling another human being, forcing him to do something against his will.

I should have...but I didn't.

In fact, I liked it a lot. Perhaps too much.

Lord, help me.

12.

I was waiting in another room when Detective Sharp returned with a glass of water and handed it to me.

He stared down at me for a moment, frowning. I peeked into his thoughts and watched him, trying to remember why he had agreed to help me further. He couldn't remember why, but it had seemed like a good idea at the time, and so he ran with it.

"Ready to roll," said Detective Sharp, perhaps a little too excitedly. I might have encouraged him to help me a bit too much. "Come to my side of the desk. Bring your chair. This could take a while."

I did as I was told, although I could probably stand all day, or all week. My legs didn't ache, nor did my muscles grow tired. I think, in fact, that my muscles regenerated and refreshed in the microseconds during use.

Such a freak.

No, came the voice from down deep. *Not a freak.*

When I sat, Detective Sharp said, "Shall we get on with it?"

"On with what?"

"The Starbucks surveillance tape."

***

These days, all surveillance tape can be downloaded as a movie file. I watched Jason rather expertly click through various screens and files until he found the one in question. It read: "Sbucks-MP-Feed1-Open" followed by the date and time.

"Have you gone over the tape?" I asked.

"Not yet."

"When did you get the case?"

"Last week, when Renaldo's case files got redistributed. Been meaning to look it over."

"What were Detective Renaldo's findings?"

"According to his notes—"

"Which you just read."

"Yes, but I'd spoken with him previously regarding the case, too. We all had. We were all confused by her disappearance. We all offered theories. Nothing panned out. Anyway, according to Renaldo, there was nothing on the tapes that seemed to indicate that she had ever left the Starbucks."

"So, she just disappeared," I said. "Poof. Off the face of the earth."

"Seems like it. Trust me, it fucked with Renaldo's head. He took the case to heart, worked on it night and day, up until the day he died."

"You mean the day he was killed."

"Right."

"So, what *is* on the tape?"

"I think it's time to find out."

He clicked on the file, and a window opened. He pressed *play* and I think we both sat forward.

"Too bad we don't have popcorn," he said.

"I wish I could eat popcorn."

"You can't eat popcorn?"

"Long story," I said.

He shrugged, and we both watched the screen.

13.

The wide-lens camera had been strategically placed.

Positioned in the parking lot at the side of the building, it provided both a wide shot of the front entrance of Starbucks and a side shot of the back door, too. One camera, both front and back doors. Nice.

A few days ago, Henry Gleason had emailed me the "missing person kit" that I always required for such cases: five recent photos, social security number, cell phone number, driver's license number, contact information for family and friends, and anything else that he thought might prove helpful.

Although I had committed Lucy Gleason's face

to memory, I had seen the tape a dozen or more times at this point. Most people in the area had. Corona Police Department had released the tape to the public, asking for leads. According to Detective Renaldo's notes, nothing had panned out. The case had gone cold with his untimely death.

So, what leads they had gathered from those anonymous calls, I didn't know. But I would, soon. I recognized her immediately when she appeared from the bottom of the frame. There she was, moving right to left, toward the Starbucks. Had I possessed a normal pulse, it probably would have quickened right about now, thumping steadily just inside my temple. Instead, there was no physical reaction to seeing her, other than my own excitement level increased.

There she is, I thought, *Lucy Gleason*, "The Disappearing Wife," as the press had dubbed her.

Of course, I had studied the video a dozen more times after taking the case, too. But the video available to me online had been only a fragment of what I was seeing now, which was the complete feed.

We'll call this, I thought, *the extended cut.*

Lucy was a thin woman. She was dressed in tight black yoga pants and pink Converse sneakers. The sneakers glittered. Her age was tough to determine, although I knew she was thirty-eight, which was getting close to my own age, although you would never know it.

The woman on the screen, the "Disappearing

Wife," seemed oblivious to the fact that she was about to disappear off the face of the earth. This was evidence for me. It was telling. She didn't seem fearful. Indeed, she even casually looked down at her cell phone at some point.

"Would give my left nut to know what she was looking at on her cell phone," said Detective Sharp.

"Too quick to read a text message," I said.

Sharp nodded. "Renaldo pulled her text records. Nothing around that time. Sent or received."

"Maybe she was looking at the time."

"Yeah, maybe."

"But you don't think so?"

"No," said Sharp. "Looks to me like she was expecting to hear from someone, and didn't. She looks, I dunno, sort of disappointed."

I was impressed with Jason Sharp. The "Disappearing Wife" was wearing sunglasses, and so there wasn't much to work with there, as far as discerning her emotions. But, admittedly, I got a sense that she had been disappointed as well. The way she exhaled slightly. The way she paused slightly in mid-step, as if she thought she had just received a message.

"I agree," I said. "Replay it."

He did, using a dial next to the keyboard. He turned it slightly, and the video went back two or three seconds and started again immediately. Yes, there it was again. She virtually jumped when she reached for her phone. And then I saw why.

"The person coming toward her," I said.

"Look."

He replayed the video again. A man, maybe twenty yards away and coming toward her, reached for his own cell phone just as she reached for hers.

"His phone rang," I said. "Or beeped or chirped."

The detective nodded. "She thought it might be hers."

"Right," I said.

"Except, of course, what are the chances his cell phone sounded like her cell phone?"

"Not a very good chance," I said.

"Which means she was jumpy," said the detective. "Reacting to any sound she heard."

"Almost as if she was nervous about something," I said.

Sharp nodded. His pointed nose waved through the air like a maestro's wand. "Or nervous about someone," he said. "Except, where does that get us?"

"Nowhere yet," I said. "But it's a start."

"A start is something."

"I agree. Can I see her text history?" I asked.

I didn't need to prompt the young detective. "Don't see why not. The wife's been missing for nearly a month now, and we've got nothing."

"You've got me," I said.

"A private dick with no di—" He caught himself.

"Good catch," I said.

"Er, sorry."

"Nothing I haven't heard before, Detective," I said. "Wanna keep watching?"

He nodded and rolled the video.

14.

We watched her cross the parking lot and enter the Starbucks with no fanfare. She didn't speak with anyone and kept her head down. Once inside, through the smoked glass, we lost track of her.

"Interior footage?" I asked.

"Wouldn't that be nice?"

I knew this, of course. Everyone knew this. I nodded.

He added, "They have since installed an interior camera. Too little, too late."

I nodded again, and for the next two hours, we watched my client appear and disappear out of the screen, going inside, searching outside, circling the building. Covering his mouth and calling loudly. He looked like a crazy man. He also looked like a man who had lost his wife.

We backtracked the video, going over it frame by frame, studying everyone coming in and going out. But no one looked like her—or even looked like her in disguise. There was no one unaccountable, either. Meaning, a man with a beard didn't suddenly emerge who hadn't already come in.

Later, the police came, searching the exterior and interior, taking statements, and taking photos.

"Police checked behind the counter, the back room, even the freezer. Everywhere. No one saw her go back there, and they had like seven employees working at the time. *Seven.* What coffee shop has seven fucking employees working at one time?"

"Is this a trick question?"

He ignored me and backtracked again. We both were taking copious notes.

"Husband doesn't come into view until..." Sharp checked his notes. "Until fourteen minutes after she goes in. Almost fifteen. If you ask me, that seems like a reasonable amount of time to come looking for your wife. It doesn't seem, you know, suspicious."

I nodded.

"The police come," he checked the notes again, "thirty-two minutes after she disappears. All normal stuff, if you ask me."

"Normal, except she hasn't been seen since."

We both stared at Henry on the screen, who was

now frozen in mid-yell, one hand cupping his mouth, the other shielding his eyes from the sun's glare. The disappearance had happened just after noon.

After a moment, Sharp said, "Husband's been taking some heat."

"Shouldn't be. It's obvious that he's at a loss, too."

"Unless he's in on something? Or unless they're in on something together."

"Magic tricks?" I asked. "Teleporting into alternate dimensions?"

"No one asked for a comedian. In fact, he hired you. You talked to him, face to face. What's your gut say?"

I decided against mentioning the fact that I had dipped inside Henry's memory and therefore, knew he was innocent. Instead, I settled for, "I believe him."

Sharp looked at me, and then gave me a short nod. "I haven't talked to him yet, but I know Renaldo wasn't too hung up on him, although..."

"Although what?"

"There was a history of violence between them."

"Oh?"

"Police were called twice in the last two years. Both times by neighbors. Both times, he was given a warning."

"No arrests?"

"No violence. According to the reports, he never

touched her. Just a lot of yelling."

"Doesn't seem like a lead," I said.

"Maybe not," he said. "But it's something."

"Something," I said, "is better than nothing."

"They teach you that in private eye school?"

"No, at the Federal Law Enforcement Training Center."

"Fancy."

I chuckled, and we stared at the monitor some more.

After a moment, Sharp asked, "Any theories yet, based on what you've seen?"

I shrugged. I might be a creature of the night, and have access to some pretty amazing talents, but I didn't know all or see all. I said, "No one suspicious came in after her. No one suspicious came out. No one carrying, say, a large plastic bag came out."

"And no one came out the back, either," he added.

Indeed, the back door had remained closed the entire time. "Any chance we missed it?"

"No way," said Sharp. "I was looking."

I was, too, of course.

"Not to mention," added Sharp, "that Renaldo went over this like a hundred times. No one came out that back door."

"Windows?"

"None. It's a corner space in a shopping center. One front door, one back door. Even the bathrooms are windowless. You ask me, a bathroom should have a fucking window."

Now that we had sat together for a few hours, Detective Sharp let go of his tough-guy act, and some of his personality was coming through.

We were silent some more. Admittedly, nothing was coming to me. No hits, no feelings, no theories, no real impressions. *No, that's not right.* I was getting one impression. And it was a big one. And the more I thought about it, the more I was sure it was right.

I think my excitement might have been obvious. The detective snapped his gaze over to me. "What is it?"

"No theories yet, Detective, but I am sure of one thing."

"And what's that?"

"She's still alive."

He looked at me long and hard. "Yeah, I'm thinking that, too."

15.

I was boxing at Jacky's gym.

Except this time, I was working out with another trainer—and a trainer who didn't seem to look too happy about working out with me.

Tough noogies.

Jacky himself working closely with my son, up in the ring. My son had wanted to come tonight. I wasn't sure how wise it was to teach a boy how to fight when he was already stronger than most kids. But I understood what was going on here: Anthony hadn't left my side for the past few months, ever since his father had died. Tammy could take me or leave me. Anthony was a different story. He shadowed me just about everywhere I went.

Tammy handled her father's loss differently.

She buried herself in books and schoolwork. She finished novels bigger and fatter than anything I'd ever read, even back in grad school. Books about divergents and tributes, featuring characters called Tris and Katness, or was it Kat and Trissness? I didn't know; either way, both had way cooler names than me.

Despite her independence, sometimes, late at night, I would hear Tammy crying softly in her room. I would then put away my files, turn off my laptop, and slip into her room unannounced. I would crawl into bed and pull her to me and listen to her cry against my shoulder until she would finally go to sleep. More than once, I fell asleep next to her, only to awaken late in the day.

The thing about a mommy who works the night shift and goes to bed at the crack of dawn—or slips into a minor coma, to be more accurate—is that a son or daughter can't, well, crawl into bed with her when they need her.

Anyway, the new trainer was holding up punching mitts, or focus mitts, before me. He held them up as I hit them harder and harder. With each punch, I watched him wince until he finally stepped back and said his hands needed a break.

I didn't doubt it. As he slipped off the mitts, I caught a fragment of his thoughts: he was wondering what drug I was on. Speed, he figured. Maybe bath salts.

With my trainer undoubtedly wishing he never showed up for work today, I sat down and watched my son work with Jacky up in the ring. Jacky was personally working out with my son, showing him proper footwork and striking techniques. Presently, he was holding my son's right arm straight, adjusting his elbow and shoulder height and wrists. I could hear Jacky's thick accent from here, barking orders. I could also see a wicked gleam in the old trainer's eye. With my son, he was liking what he was seeing.

Tammy turned to books, while Anthony turned to me.

As the weeks passed, he grew more and more attached to me. Often, he would slip into my office, nonchalantly, quietly, almost secretly. One moment I would be working, the next, I would look up and he would be there. It was a credit to his own supernatural prowess that he could sneak up on me, perhaps one of the few people who could.

Mostly, he would play on his Gameboy or pretend to read a book. I knew he was pretending because he never actually turned the pages. Sometimes, he would come in and talk, usually about nothing important. He would ramble. Other times, he would come in and sit quietly, staring down at his hands. I asked him if there was anything I could do for him, or help him with, or if he wanted to do something together, and the answer was invariably "no."

That is, until this evening, when I found him sitting in my office, holding a book he didn't bother trying to read. The title was *Beautiful Creatures*, which might have been a movie, too, although we hadn't seen it. I was pretty sure that was his sister's book.

As I shut down my computer, I asked if he wanted to go to boxing with me and, wonder of wonders, he had perked up immediately. I smiled, relieved that I had finally, *finally* found something that interested him.

Now, I almost regretted it.

Almost.

Then again, maybe my son did need to know how to fight. Maybe being who he is—the strongest kid in his school—would prompt older boys to test him, to prove their own worth, to show that a younger kid wasn't tougher than them.

I hoped my son wouldn't use his growing strength for ill. I hoped I wasn't creating a supervillain here, although that thought nearly made me giggle.

My son had a good heart, and he was a boy hurting and lost, and looking for someone to connect with. For a while, I had been that someone. Boy, had I been. From following me out to the laundry room, to sitting with me in the office.

Now, as I watched my son, something curious was happening: he wasn't looking at me. No, Jacky had his full attention. And, more amazingly, he had Jacky's full attention, too.

I saw something even stranger, something I wasn't prepared for: as they moved together in this boxing dance of theirs, as Anthony delivered slow-motion punches and as Jacky corrected his technique, I saw their two auras do something I had rarely, if ever, seen.

Their auras had somehow connected. Where Anthony's aura ended and Jacky's began, I didn't know. Never had I seen this before. The auras looked, at least to my eyes, to be one big aura.

What the devil?

I sat forward in one of the many plastic chairs that lined the perimeter of the gym and actually rubbed my eyes, but there was no rubbing away this strange display.

Yes, I could see auras. From what I understood, all vampires could see auras. Auras were the energy field that surrounded our bodies. And not just the energy, but, some claimed, our souls themselves, which were too big to be contained by flesh and bones.

I knew Jacky had lost his own son years ago to a drug overdose, and I always suspected that he coached and trained these kids here to fill a void. My suspicions were confirmed with my son. Their connection was tangible. Hell, *spiritual*.

What's happening? I wondered.

I didn't know, but with my own trainer long gone—in fact, I'd seen him slip out the front door with nary a glance back—I suspected that Jacky just might have found himself a new protégé.

And, as Jacky reached over and mussed my son's hair—with Anthony grinning from ear to ear, his first grin in months—I suspected Jacky had

found much more.
 They both had.

16.

I was with the Librarian, a man who might not be a man, and a man who might not really exist, at least in this physical world.

Who he was remained a mystery. That he had once been an ordinary human, I had no doubt. How he existed now, I didn't know, although his knowledge of alchemy might explain a lot. What it explained, I didn't know, since I didn't know much about alchemy, other than a book I'd read years ago by Paulo Coelho, a book that, at the time, had been meaningless to me.

"Paulo touched on real truths," said the Librarian.

Although Maximus, aka the Librarian, was immortal, he and I had an open telepathic line of communication. Not so much with other immortals, who were closed off to me. With that said, Max and I generally spoke aloud, rather than communicate telepathically. I liked speaking aloud. Call me old fashioned, but speaking aloud was what *normal* people did. I needed to do what normal people did, as often as possible.

He continued, "Some books you are ready for, some you are not. You were not ready for *The Alchemist*, although it laid the groundwork to open your mind."

"What do you mean?"

"You had not awakened, Sam. You were closed, asleep. Life was as it was expected to be, with little questioning on your end. Now you question much and seek deeper answers."

"And *The Alchemist* helped do that?"

"That, along with your attack many years ago. But not everyone needs to be rendered immortal to awaken. There are many paths to greater truths."

"And why should we seek greater truths?"

"There's no 'shoulds' in this world, Sam. There is only following your heart, your own truths, and explore where they lead you."

"Well, they led me here, to talk to you."

"And so they have. You have a question for me, I see."

"I do. It's about my son."

Max nodded once, long and slow, from behind his "help desk" counter within the Occult Reading Room, itself filled with hundreds, if not thousands, of very old and very strange-looking books, many of which were, if you asked me, downright dangerous.

The Occult Reading Room was a secret room located on the third floor of Cal State Fullerton's epic library, a room that few knew about, and even fewer actually saw. *Secret* may not have been the correct word. There were, after all, actual books in this reading room, books that were even referenced in the library's computer database.

"Although referenced," he said, "few would think to look for them, and fewer still have heard of them."

"But if they have heard of them, and they look for it..."

"Then I am always here."

"Always?"

"A figure of speech. But more or less, yes. You can mostly find me here."

That such a young-looking guy could be so wise was still something I was getting used to. I said, "The emerald medallion was used to give my son back his humanity, correct?"

"Correct."

"But he also retained some of his supernatural traits."

"This appears to be so."

"He seems to have retained all the good supernatural traits," I said. "And none of the bad."

"Again, yes."

The Librarian watched me through eyes that

never judged and were always kind. I was reminded of a newborn's eyes, full of wonder and peace and joy. I was not used to such eyes. His were a pleasant change of pace, and if I wasn't careful, I could get lost in those eyes.

I asked, "Then how is the diamond medallion any different?"

"It's not, Sam, although it is obvious now that even I cannot predict the reaction each person will have to the medallions."

The four medallions were, of course, created by the Librarian, relics put into place to help creatures like me combat the things within. That all four of the relics had gravitated toward me was something I didn't yet understand. They surely could have landed in the lap of other creatures of the night. In fact, I knew of one such vampire—an ancient vampire—who had spent quite a long time looking for the emerald medallion.

I gathered my thoughts, thinking them aloud. "The emerald medallion didn't just give my son back his mortality, but enabled him to keep some of his immortal powers, too."

"It appears so, Samantha," said the Librarian. "But we cannot know that it was the medallion that gave him these gifts...or if it was something else."

"What do you mean?"

"I'm not sure what I mean, Sam. Your son's reaction to the medallion was unexpected."

"And you suspect...something else might be involved?"

"In a word, yes."

"And you are just telling me this now?"

"I've only recently deduced this...and I knew you would be back sooner rather than later."

"Should I be concerned?" I asked. "About my son?"

He shook his head and his kind eyes seemed to smile. "No, Sam. But there is something else at play here, something—or perhaps someone—who has helped your son greatly. This something or someone is beyond even my own perception."

"That sounds frightening," I said.

"It doesn't have to be, Sam. Your son, it appears, is in good hands."

"But whose hands?" I asked.

"That, as the old game show hosts used to say, is the million-dollar question. As of now, yes, the emerald medallion behaved very similarly to the diamond medallion, which not only returns your mortality, but also helps you retain all the perks, if you will. That is, all the perks of your choosing."

"My choosing?"

"Yes."

"I could retain...my great strength?"

"Yes, that, and more."

"My psychic ability?"

"Yes."

"More?" I asked.

"Much more, Sam."

I thought about what could be much more...and gasped. "Flying?"

He nodded slowly. "Yes, Sam. You would retain that, as well."

"And all this without the bloodsucking and sleeping during the day?"

"Yes, Sam. No more blood."

"And I could finally see myself in the mirror and have normal nails again?"

"Yes, Sam."

How Fang presently owned the fourth and final medallion was another story—a story I didn't presently know. After all, how he came upon the diamond medallion, why he wore it, and what he even knew about it were all questions whose answers were unknown to me. A part of me wondered if he even knew what he had, if he understood the value of the relic that presently hung around his neck.

Maybe, maybe not. Either way, he and I were going to have a long talk...and soon.

"And what of the dark master within me?" I asked. "Does the diamond medallion eradicate her as well?"

He smiled down on me. "Completely."

"And no such creature resides within my son?"

"No, Sam. The emerald medallion took care of that, as well."

"This is all very weird."

"It's a weird universe, Samantha."

I sighed and continued standing there. I found that I was hugging myself. After a moment, Maximus said, "But you didn't come here today to talk about medallions, did you?"

"No," I said, shaking my head. "My son..." But as soon as I began the sentence, the words got caught in my throat, and emotions poured out of me in tears, and the next thing I knew the Librarian had his arms around my shoulders, pulling me into his shoulder.

After a long moment of this, still unable to speak, the Librarian's thoughts appeared in my head, just inside my ears.

Your son and the boxer remember each other on a soul level.

A soul level?

Many lifetimes ago, they were deeply connected as father and son, as they have been often in many lives, in many places.

But Anthony had a different dad...

In this lifetime, Sam. But the boxer, Jacky, and your son, Anthony, made an agreement to connect again, in this life, if your boy was ever lost or sad or lonely.

I wept harder into the Librarian's shoulder and he squeezed me tighter.

There is deep love between them, Sam. Both need each other.

I nodded, and finally couldn't even form words to think, let alone speak. Instead, I buried myself deeper into the young man's shoulder. A young man who was, in fact, ancient, and wept for my son.

17.

I was back at the 'Bucks, as Tammy called it.

The evening shift would be rolling in soon, which was why I was here now. Jasmine Calcutta, who had, perhaps, the most exotic name I'd ever heard, would be here soon, and she was expecting me. We had planned on meeting fifteen minutes before her shift.

I had just sat down with a venti water on the rocks, when I saw a young girl appear at the entrance, blinking and looking around. She was wearing a green Starbucks apron. I waved to her and she nodded and came over.

"Can I get you a coffee?" I asked.

"Thanks, but I'm a little coffeed out," said Jasmine Calcutta.

"Coffeed out," I said. "The two words that keep Starbucks executives up at night. Well, that and their Sumatra Roast."

She giggled and sat down opposite me. "That was kind of funny."

"My kids don't think I'm funny. They think I'm embarrassing."

She giggled again, and I think we were hitting it off. Hitting it off with a witness is always a good thing. Much better than the alternative. Jasmine Calcutta was maybe twenty-five. Her eyes, I think, were violet, which surprised the hell out of me. The girl with the most exotic name might also have had the most exotic eyes I'd ever seen. Some girls got all the breaks.

"You're a private investigator," she said.

"I am. But you can call me Sam."

"A real private investigator?"

"In the flesh," I said.

"Do you have, like, a license or something?"

"I do."

"Can I, like, see it?"

She wanted to see it out of curiosity's sake, not because she doubted me. I didn't need to be a mind reader to see that. I produced it from my purse and she *oohed* and *ahed* at it for a few seconds before handing it back.

"So cool," she said. "I want to do something like that."

I pointed to my license photo, in which I might have been wearing too much makeup. "You mean take great pictures?"

She giggled again. "No. Be a private detective. A real one, like you."

"Well, here's your chance to watch a real detective at work."

She nodded enthusiastically.

I said, "I need you to do your best to remember everything you can about Lucy Gleason."

"I'll try, but it's kind of getting fuzzier and fuzzier."

"Real detectives don't use words like fuzzier," I said.

"Okay, sorry."

"I'm teasing, Jasmine."

"Oh, right, sorry."

"No need to be sorry," I said. "Just give me your hands."

"My hands?"

"Yes."

"Why?"

"It's a super-secret interview trick I learned."

"Wow, really?"

"Really." I then directed this thought to her: *It feels perfectly normal to give your hands to the nice, if not beautiful, lady and do whatever she asks.*

She cocked her head to one side, and then nodded once.

I'm a monster, I thought. A monster who needed answers. I gestured for her hands and she presented them to me from across the table.

I slipped mine over hers and asked her to close her eyes and think back to the day Lucy disappeared. Luckily, most of the Starbuckians were too absorbed with their laptops and their own self-importance to notice two women holding hands in the coffee shop. Additionally, I had found a table that wasn't in direct line with her fellow co-workers, who might wonder what we were doing.

I didn't want to make a scene, so I held her hands discreetly, just like two friends visiting together, sharing a sweet moment. Or, heck, praying together. Why not?

We weren't two friends and we most certainly weren't praying; instead, I was employing the same technique I had used with Henry Gleason, my client. Except Henry's memory had been fresh and vivid and full of charged emotion, which had heightened his remembrance.

Now, as I held her hands, I asked her to tell me anything that she could remember from that day. She nodded, her eyes still closed.

And just as she opened her mouth to speak, I was inside her mind, completely and thoroughly...

***

"It was just like any other day, you know," she began, and as she spoke those words, images appeared in her thoughts, images I was now privy to, as well. In her mind's eye, I saw a very different scene in Starbucks. Yes, I was reliving these memories right along with her, without her knowing it. It's good to be me.

Sometimes.

Yes, we were in this very same Starbucks but, instead of it being evening, the day was bright, at a time when I would have been just been getting up—a miserable, painful time of day for me. On this day, Jasmine had been working an earlier shift, and she distinctly remembered watching Lucy Gleason come in.

"We were busy, but not Starbucks busy," she said.

"Starbucks is an adjective now?" I asked. "Never mind. It's just a rhetorical question. Continue."

She answered anyway. "Well, we have different levels of busy, at least here. Starbucks busy is our busiest, since it can get crazy in here, especially in the mornings and especially on the weekends."

"So, it wasn't Starbucks busy," I said. "Got it."

The scene continued in her mind, and I continued following it with much interest.

"You have to remember, Sam," she said. "We have thousands and thousands of customers a week. Days go by in a blur. Heck, hours go by in a blur."

"I can imagine," I said. "Starbucks busy."

"Right," she said.

Luckily, she did remember some of that day. She had to, because she had been forced to recall what had happened, especially after being questioned repeatedly by the police. For her, it wasn't just another day. For her, it stood out. Sadly, there were still missing chunks in her memory. That was not unexpected. Some claimed that the subconscious remembers everything a person sees. However, that hadn't been my experience when I'd occasionally plumbed people for their memories. No, I didn't go around doing this often. In fact, very little. But the few people I had done this with, I had seen whole chunks of missing memory. Empty spaces filled with nonsense.

That was what I was seeing here: people coming and going, their faces vague, their bodies amorphous, their orders blurring into the next order. Then Jasmine had a gap filled by other memories, other people, and other places and times. I saw who I suspected was her boyfriend. I saw things I really didn't need to see. Then I saw a woman who was clearly her mother. She smiled often at her. All of these superfluous memories were interwoven with the main thread, which was that day in Starbucks.

That fateful day.

***

Jasmine is working the register. People come and go. Money is exchanged, credit cards are swiped, gift cards are used. The door opens, and Jasmine looks up and greets the customer, as any good Starbucks employee should.

There she is.

"Welcome to Starbucks," I hear Jasmine say.

Lucy Gleason nods and appears to say something, but Jasmine's wandering mind fills in the gap with an image of her boyfriend riding a dirt bike, shirtless.

Now, Lucy Gleason is waiting in line behind two other people.

Here, Jasmine's memory is fuzzy at best. The snatches that she recalls of Lucy waiting in line are brief and chaotic, and that's to be expected. Still, every now and then, Jasmine's eyes land on Lucy...and for good reason. Lucy is chewing her nails nervously, and looking around. In particular, she's looking up.

She's looking for cameras.

Now, Lucy's head snaps around quickly, looking behind her, and this also catches Jasmine's attention.

In a blur, the two people before Lucy come and go, and now it's her turn to order. Lucy steps up.

"What can we make for you?" asks Jasmine.

Lucy doesn't look her in the eye. Instead, she cracks her neck a little, then reaches back and rubs it. Nervous, stressed. "Just a water for now."

"Sure," says Jasmine cheerily enough. "Can I get you anything else?"

The image in Jasmine's memory is briefly replaced by another face, another time, another customer. That Jasmine has remembered this much from a brief encounter with thousands of customers is amazing enough. This other customer fades away, to be replaced again by Lucy, who is now walking away.

Jasmine briefly watches her go, before the image fades away. It was, of course, where Lucy was clearly going that got my attention.

She had been headed to the bathrooms.

***

I released Jasmine's hands.

"And that's all I remember," she was saying.

"You can open your eyes now," I said, aware that she was still mostly under the command of my voice, which did little for me, but excited the bitch within me.

Jasmine opened her eyes slowly, and seemed to return to the present. She blinked hard, and then, opened her eyes wide.

"Wow, what happened? I felt like I was asleep—"

"You won't make a scene," I said evenly, keeping my voice low. I could have just as easily thought the words, but we were isolated enough, and there was enough ambient noise that I couldn't have been overheard.

She nodded minutely, blinked slowly, and said, "I really don't remember much. She ordered a water, and then went to the bathroom."

"And you never saw her again?"

"No,"

"Never saw her exit?"

Jasmine shook her head. "If she did, I didn't see

it. We don't monitor the bathrooms here. There are no keys or anything. People just come and go, and the bathrooms are around the corner, sort of out of my sight from the cash register."

"Did you see her pick up the water?"

She thought hard, and then shook her head. "I don't remember."

"That's okay," I said. "Thank you."

"Sorry I wasn't of much help," she said. She looked at her cell phone. "I have to get to work. My shift starts soon."

I thanked her and watched her go, all too aware that controlling her had been very, very exciting.

Too exciting.

18.

I sipped on my water and considered what I'd learned.

Jasmine Calcutta's statement lined up perfectly with what she had given the police. After all, like Henry Gleason, I'd witnessed her experience firsthand.

And what had I witnessed?

Lucy had been nervous, that much was certain. She had looked over her shoulder more than once. She had looked for a camera, too. She hadn't ordered an iced mocha, but I knew that, too. She had told Henry she wanted an iced mocha, and had come in and ordered a water. The iced mochas were, in fact, a ruse. Almost immediately, Lucy had gone straight to the restrooms.

Had she actually made it to the restrooms? Did she meet someone, say, in the short hallway?

There was no way to know, since Jasmine's memory stopped just as Lucy entered the short hallway to the restrooms.

I drummed my long, pointed nails on the mostly clean table. My drumming was a tad louder than I'd intended it to be, so I stopped. Damned, big-ass nails. Finally, I got up and headed to the bathrooms. Knowing they may have been Lucy's final destination, I decided to investigate the bathrooms anew, with renewed vigor and interest.

Lucky me.

There was little spirit activity at Starbucks, outside of the occasional grandparent or parent or friend swinging by a loved one to say hi. Murders and suicides tended to result in real hauntings. Although violent acts didn't result in hauntings, they almost indelibly left their imprint on the environment.

But I saw nothing. No chaotic, staticy energy. Nothing. Normal energy. Peaceful energy. Starbucks energy.

Whatever that meant.

One thing was certain: no violent act had been perpetrated here. No one had been killed or raped or beaten here, as far as I could see.

Although this Starbucks was a little older than others, it still had that hip, industrial, modern vibe that people loved so much. That Starbucks feel, if you will.

The hallway was short, lined with wood paneling and photographs of Huntington Beach Pier. There was a broom closet that had, yes, a broom, a mop and a bucket in it, along with a water heater. No room for a female adult, even a small female adult like Lucy Gleason. I shut the broom closet door and moved on.

To my right was the men's restroom. Directly ahead was the women's. I tried the handle to the women's, unlocked. I stepped inside, feeling more excited than I should have about going into a public bathroom.

***

The bathroom light turned on automatically.

I wasn't sure what I was looking for. The bathroom, of course, looked exactly the same as it had last time. But she had come here last, dammit.

Here, in this bathroom. I was sure of it.

I had seen it!

I noted the shining metal trashcan, the low, sleek toilet, a sink, a mirror and a baby-changing station. I unlatched the baby-changing station, opening and closing the plastic tray. It worked as it should. There was nothing hidden behind it, no secret panel.

With that thought in mind, I checked the mirror carefully; it, too, was sealed to the wall. I could pry it loose and give a look behind it, but what good would that do? The sucker had been on the wall for a long time.

I turned in the small circle. Outside of disappearing down into the toilet, I was at a loss.

Stumped.

Confounded.

I hated that.

I sighed, looked at myself in the mirror, and saw mostly nothing. I had added some quick foundation this evening, eyeliner, just enough so that I would show up in most reflections, most mirrors, most security cameras. However, I could see where I had missed some spots. An empty spot was there on my forehead, as if I had a hole in my head.

I held up my hands...and couldn't see them. I pressed them against the cold mirror, and neither a smudge nor a fingerprint remained.

This was, of course, nothing new to me, other than another reminder to how far I had slipped from the realm of normal...to that of the paranormal.

I sighed and considered where the devil Lucy had gone, and decided to head for the men's bathroom next.

Might as well.

19.

"Someone's in here," called a man's voice when I tried the handle and found it locked.

Feeling awkward, I leaned a shoulder against the wall opposite the door, folded my arms and waited. While I waited, a middle-aged guy stepped into the hallway, whistling to himself. He stopped whistling, looked at me, looked up at the nameplate on the door, and frowned.

"The women's is broken," I said.

He nodded and slid into line next to me.

"Is it going to be bad in there?" I asked.

He was a balding guy with a nice build. He wore a Lakers tank top and basketball shorts. He chuckled and said, "It's hit or miss."

"Literally," I said.

He grinned. "Something like that. But it's Starbucks, so..."

"So, it's Starbucks clean."

"I'm not sure what that means."

"Neither do I." And since I had nothing better to do, I took a shot in the dark, which might not be any different than what was going on in the men's bathroom. "Weird about that girl disappearing here."

"Oh, right. Heard about that."

"Apparently, she was last seen going into the bathroom."

He raised an eyebrow. "Okay, now you're freaking me out."

I laughed. "Sorry."

"I'm just trying to take a piss here."

"Me, too. But girls call it peeing."

"Yeah, right. Sorry. Didn't mean to—"

"Just busting your balls, bub. So, what do you think happened to that girl?"

"I would say the husband did her in."

"Except the husband never came inside, and she was last seen inside."

"Last seen by who?"

I nodded toward the counter. "One of the girls working the cash register."

"I dunno, man."

"Woman."

"Well, either way, it's a fu—freakin' mystery."

"If you were hired to look into it, where would you begin?"

"Why are you asking?"

I showed him my private investigator's license, complete with a face doused in makeup. "That's why I'm asking."

"Oh, shit. You're a private cop?"

"Yup."

"And you're looking into this?"

"Yup."

"You really don't have to use the bathroom, do you?"

"Nope."

The door opened, and he jumped in front of me and turned back. "Cause I really do gotta go, um, potty. Sorry!"

And he slammed the door in my face.

***

He came out five minutes later, drying his hands, thank God.

"Hey, I cleaned up in there a little for you."

"You are a good man."

"You have no idea."

"I have a ten-year-old boy and was married for nearly a dozen years. Guys miss. Often."

He laughed and motioned for me to follow him. "Come here, I wanna show you something."

"If I had a nickel for every time a guy at Starbucks told me they wanted to show me something in the bathroom..."

"Just come on, smartass. Check this out."

He led me inside. It was an exact replica of the women's restroom, complete with the baby-changing station. There was, however, one noticeable difference: the smell of urine. Also, there were one, two, three instances of graffiti, although minor at that. A pencil drawing of a man's genitalia here, a pen drawing above the toilet that said "Shit here," complete with an arrow. Helpful.

"So, I was cleaning the floor a little—"

"Cleaning the floor?"

"I have OCD, what can I say? Anyway, I was using a bunch of paper towels, pushing them around with my foot—"

"Why?"

"You seem like a classy chick, and I don't want you to think all guys are slobs."

"That's sweet," I said. "I still think all guys are slobs. All guys, except maybe you."

"Better than nothing," he said.

"I might have to marry you."

He held up his left hand. "Someone beat you to it."

"Oh, damn. Then can I hire you to clean my house?"

"You couldn't afford me."

I laughed. He laughed. I said, "So, what did you want to show me?"

"Well, I was mopping under the sink when my toe hit something."

"Hit what?"

"Watch."

He used his foot to reach under the sink and tap on the wall vent. Nothing happened at first. He tapped again, and the vent fell away, hanging in place by a single screw.

"Voila," he said, and pointed.

I saw it, too.

It was an opening behind the wall.

An opening big enough for a very small person.

"Please tell me there's not a dead body in there," I said. Of course, the idea of a dead body in there didn't disturb me at all. If anything, it intrigued me mightily.

"I checked, it's empty."

"Big enough to hold a person?"

"You tell me."

"Give me some room," I said, and dropped down to my knees. "Is the door locked behind us?"

"Let me check." He checked. "Yes."

"Good," I said from under the sink. I felt my excitement rising. At least the floor was semi-clean, thanks to Mr. OCD.

I used my index finger to pry loose the remaining screw holding the vent in place. My nails might look hideous, but they did occasionally serve a purpose. I set the vent aside and peered into the dark opening. Behind me, Mr. Clean was peering over my shoulder, too.

"Seems small," he said.

I studied the dimensions, my voice echoing within the dusty, dark opening. "I could fit."

"I sure as hell couldn't."

"You're also not a missing housewife who is, I think, even smaller than me."

"Except she's not in there."

"Good point," I said. I stood suddenly and shoved Captain Obvious hard against the bathroom wall, somewhere between the sink and the door. I pinned him to the wall.

"Hey, what the fu—"

I said, "You will forget me, the bathroom, and especially the vent. Oh, and you will forget me feeding from you, as well."

"I...okay."

I took his hand, made a slit across the inside of his wrist, and drank deeply from the man, all while he stared down at me in dumbfounded shock. I stared up at him, looking, I'm sure, like the ghoul that I knew I was.

When I had drunk my fill—a bloody latte, if you will—I released his hand.

"Now," I said, wiping the corners of my mouth and licking my own fingers. "You will forget all of this." I looked at his wrist, which was already healing nicely. "Now, go."

And he went, confused, blinking rapidly. At the open door, he looked back at me once, blinked fast, and then was gone.

Now, said a voice in my head, a voice that didn't belong to me. *That wasn't so hard, was it?*

No, I thought. *Not hard at all.*

20.

I was sitting with Detective Sharp at a Carl's Jr., a popular fast food chain here in Southern California. At least, it was popular to flesh-eating mortals, of which there were, apparently, many.

Detective Sharp was looking at me curiously as he worked his way through a hamburger that would have fed my entire family. Or would have fed them back in the day. The burger was called the Six-Dollar Burger. The catch being, of course, was that it was only $3.95. Brilliant advertising. You're getting more than what you're paying for. It also implied that you were getting a restaurant-quality burger without the restaurant price.

"You're expecting me to believe that she hid in a vent in the men's bathroom?" said the detective, after a few minutes of chewing. He had mostly swallowed when he spoke.

"Maybe not the men's bathroom," I said. "The women's has an identical vent under the sink."

He took another healthy bite from his burger. Admittedly, it looked like a six-dollar burger. It also looked delicious. What I wouldn't give to—

"Then go buy one," said Sharp.

Oops. He'd read my mind. I guess the detective and I were getting a little closer. I immediately placed my internal wall around me.

I said, "I dunno. Six bucks seems too much for a burger..."

"They're not really six bucks," said Sharp. "They're like three ninety-five or something. Four bucks."

I shook my head. "Says right there on the sign. Six bucks."

"It's called a six-dollar burger, but it's really four bucks."

"I'm so confused."

"Look, it's not really six—oh, you're fucking with me."

"Ya think?"

"Screw you, Samantha Moon," he said, but laughed.

I said, "Looks good, but I'm on a diet."

"What kind of diet?"

"Liquid diet."

"Suit yourself, but this is damn good."

"I'll remember it for next time. The six-dollar

burger that isn't six dollars."

He shook his head, reached for some fries. "So, these vents in the bathrooms...you think a woman could fit in them?"

I nodded. "I know I could, but not comfortably, and I wouldn't want to stay in there long—or at all. But yeah."

"And, is it safe to assume there was no woman in it now, dead or otherwise?"

"It's safe to assume it."

"Any indication that someone had, you know, been in it?"

"Nothing that I could visually confirm. Her fingerprints might be there, though."

"Yours, too, I assume."

I didn't, of course, leave fingerprints behind anymore. To do so implied I had oils on my skin, oils that transferred from my skin to say, metal. No such oils existed in me. No, I hadn't seen any signs of prints, but that was often hard to tell with the naked eye. Even a supernatural naked eye.

I said, "I was careful not to leave any prints behind. My guess, though, is that she would have cleaned it thoroughly."

"Why?"

"To leave no sign. To give the illusion that she truly disappeared."

"Not to mention, she was in a bathroom. She might have had plenty of time to clean up behind her."

"There's that," I said.

"So, what do you want me to do?" he asked.

"You know what to do," I said.

He shook his head. He didn't like it. The idea seemed preposterous to him, but he finally acquiesced. "Fine. I'll send a team over, ASAP. Hell, we've got nothing else to go on." He paused, set down his burger. "Was there any sign of force?"

"No sign of force. No blood that I could see. No scrape marks, no hair, nothing left behind."

"So, you're saying she went in there willingly?"

"That would be my guess," I said.

"This is getting crazier and crazier."

"I do crazy well."

"Well, I don't. I like things neat. I like things explainable. I like things to make sense. This makes no sense."

"Not now," I said. "But it might. Someday."

He sighed and picked up his burger.

I tried not to drool.

21.

Kingsley and I were having dinner.

While he ate and I slurped idly at the blood that pooled around my very rare steak, I found myself eyeballing the cute waiter. I wondered what I would say to lure him into the bathroom, since that had worked so well back at the Starbucks. That I still hadn't felt guilty about attacking him should have concerned me, but it didn't.

"You've got that look in your eye, Samantha Moon," said Kingsley. He had just bitten into a healthy bite of steak, and so, I had the pleasure of seeing the half-masticated meat in his mouth. He might be a power attorney during the day, but he was all animal at night. At least, around me. Good thing he couldn't read my thoughts. Most immortals couldn't.

"I imagine I do."

"You don't even hide it now? Tsk-tsk. How far you have fallen."

"Hide who I am?"

He set his fork down and momentarily paused in his chewing. Then he reached for a frosted glass of beer and drained it. Yeah, the man was an animal. Had we been dining in his spacious home, he would have wiped the back of his hand across his mouth. Instead, he used a napkin, and didn't seem happy about it.

"Well, the Samantha I know and love was a fighter. She didn't give into the cravings."

"Well, that Samantha was weak."

"I beg to differ. She was the strongest I'd ever seen. Which is why I loved her...and love her still to this day."

The demon within me recoiled at his words. "You're making me sick." Had I said those words, or had *she*?

"The Samantha that I know and love is a mom, a friend, a damn fine investigator, and, most of all, unshakeable in her belief in the inherent good within herself. Within most of us."

The big oaf was pissing me off now. Royally pissing me off. Who the fuck was he to judge me?

"The Samantha I know would have listened to criticism with an open mind. She wouldn't be fighting herself, even now, from leaping over the table and strangling me in public."

"I hate you," I said.

"No, you don't, Sam. The creature within you hates me. Hates love. Hates all that is good in your life."

"You're not good in my life. You're not good for me at all. You're a fucking cheater."

I had raised my voice. People were staring at us. Kingsley didn't care. He reached across the table and took my hand. Or tried to. Instead, faster than I had any right to move, faster than even he was prepared for, I flipped my fork around, caught it in mid-air, and drove it down through the back of his hand, impaling him and it to the wooden table.

"Go fuck yourself, asshole," I said, and got up and left.

Behind me, someone screamed.

***

We were in his oversized SUV.

I'd been crying for the past twenty minutes while Kingsley wrapped his meaty arms around me and rubbed my shoulders.

Had he been able to read my mind, he would have known what was going on, why I had lashed out, and why I had impaled his hand to the table. Then he could have explained it all to me, because I still didn't know what the hell had happened.

When the waterworks were finally done, and I was reduced to a sniffling mess, I heard a curious sound.

It was chuckling.

Kingsley was laughing to himself, even as he continued rubbing my shoulder—yes, with the very hand that I had stabbed, no less.

"What's so funny?" I asked looking up. We were in the Mulberry Street parking lot, which was part of a bigger chain of parking lots for lots of other local businesses. Many of the cars parked near the restaurant had left quickly over the past twenty minutes.

I suspected I knew why.

"You should have seen the looks on their faces," said Kingsley, and now he was chuckling louder. "One woman—" and now, Kingsley quit rubbing my shoulders, and retracted his hand. He needed his hands because he was now holding his belly. "One woman fainted right there in the restaurant." Now, Kingsley was wheezing, fighting for breath.

Damn it, his booming laughter was infectious. Hell, the whole SUV was shaking. I found myself giggling at first. Mostly, I was laughing at *him*.

"She, literally," he gasped, tears streaming down his face, "toppled right out of her chair—*splat* on the floor."

And now, for the next two minutes or so, Kingsley was laughing so hard that he couldn't speak. Worse, I found myself laughing, as well. Not quite as hard as Kingsley.

"And then, and then she looks up from the floor—" Kingsley didn't sound like Kingsley. He sounded like a wheezing, asthmatic school kid. He tried again. "And then, she looks up from the floor just as I pull the fork out of my hand—and faints again."

And now, I lost it again, completely and totally, gasping and kicking his feet. I got myself under control a lot faster than he did. I said, "That poor lady. Is she okay?"

"Yes," he said, still laughing. "The floor had carpet."

That set him off again, and I waited for him to get some control over himself. "Okay," he said, gasping, gulping air. "I think I'm done. But no guarantees."

I shook my head. "How's your hand?"

"Ah, hell, it's fine. You know that."

"Jesus, it wasn't silver was it?"

"Naw, and even if it was, it wouldn't have done any real harm."

"I'm not sure what got into me. I'm sorry."

"Oh, I know what got in you, Sam. Or what's in you now, more accurately." Kingsley sat back and wiped his eyes. That he filled the seat to overflowing went without saying. "It's in me, too. Or something similar."

"Except yours comes out each month," I said.

"Yes," said Kingsley. "And that seems sufficient for it for now."

"She wants to possess me fully. That's her goal. I know it. I can feel it."

Kingsley nodded, suddenly somber, although his eyes still twinkled in the ambient lights.

"It's usually the way, Sam."

"Then how do vampires fight their own demons?" I asked.

Kingsley looked at me sideways, looked at me long and hard, his thick hair piled up on his beefy shoulders. "Most don't, Sam. Most succumb."

"I didn't want to hear that."

"But some also come to an agreement, I think."

"What type of agreement?" I asked.

"They let the inner demon out, so to speak. But only sometimes."

"They let it control them?"

"Yes. For some, it's the only way to have peace."

"She's not controlling me," I said. "Not ever. This one, this one is different. Powerful. She's looking for a crack. All she needs is a crack. If she finds it...I don't think I'll ever come back."

Kingsley nodded, listening, still breathing hard from his outburst. "Some demons are more powerful than others. Some have other agendas."

"What does that mean?"

"She might have a reason to be inside you, whatever that might be."

"Like she picked me, on purpose?"

"Maybe, Sam. I don't know. But trust your instincts. Don't let her out, fight her."

"I'm trying." I took in some air. "I mean, I have to. I have kids, a career. I have a sister, a family. I can't let this...psychotic bitch...loose. Who knows what the hell would happen?"

"Agreed," he said.

"I have no idea what she is capable of, who she might hurt. I have no idea if I would ever be me again."

"I understand, Sam. Perhaps better than most. I, too, have a fear that I may never return. That I would stay chained to the walls of my own mind."

I shook my head. "Fuck her. She's not going to win. She's not getting out. Ever."

He reached over and gripped my hand tightly. I let him, and we held hands like that in his oversized SUV, an SUV that just might have been tilting slightly to one side—his side. After a long moment, he said, "I think we might need to find a new restaurant."

"I think so, too."

"Do you want to come over tonight?"

"We're friends, remember?"

"Friends can still come over."

"I suspect your intentions are more than friendly."

"My only intention is to hold you tight."

"I need to go," I said, and attempted to pull free, but his big, ogre-like hands anchored mine.

"I still love you, Sam," he said, "and I'm sorry for hurting you."

I worked my hands free.

"I need to go," I said, and left his SUV.

22.

We were at Hero's.

No, it wasn't the same without the cute bartender with the shark teeth hanging around his neck, but it was still our hangout. It was also one of the few places where my sister and I got to relax together. Where we could be ourselves. In hushed voices, of course. No kids. No men. No work. Just sisters. That one was mortal and one was immortal was irrelevant. Not here, not in this place. A safe place.

That one sister got *mortal* and *immortal* confused was just, well, plain cute.

Only this time, Mary Lou wasn't saying much. We were sitting in the far corner along the crowded bar, where we usually sat. A post separated us from the person next to us, which was perfect.

"You're still mad," I said. We were both nearly halfway through our first glasses of wine and she still hadn't said much. In fact, I was pretty certain she hadn't said a thing...or looked at me for that matter.

Seeing her now, the way she set her jaw, the way her left knee bounced agitatedly, reminded me our fights when we were young. Mary Lou could hold a grudge with the best of them. It was always, always, my job to break the ice. I either broke it...or I got the jaw and knee business.

"How was your day?" I asked. I didn't want the jaw or knee business. I needed my big sister. *Badly.*

"Fine."

"Anything exciting happen at work?"

"No."

"You're telling me, in that big insurance office of yours, not even one person had a birthday today?"

"No, Sam."

"Well, any meltdowns?" I asked. "Someone's always having a meltdown at your—"

"No, Sam."

"Where did you go for lunch?"

"I didn't eat lunch."

"You should really eat lunch."

"Oh my God, you're driving me crazy."

"That's what sisters do."

"No, they don't. And they especially don't keep secrets from each other."

"Can you trust me when I say that there are some secrets you might want me to keep from you?"

She looked at me, that jawline of her still rippling. If she wasn't careful, she might crack a molar. That she didn't catch that thought was, of course, the source of her irritation. Mary Lou and I had always been close. Best friends throughout our lives. Sometimes, we were closer than other times. But always, always, she was there for me.

Now, of course, she felt left out, and I didn't blame her.

"We weren't keeping secrets from you, Mary Lou."

"Then you were making fun of me, laughing at me behind my back, or inside your heads or whatever."

"We weren't laughing at you, either," I said. At least, I didn't think we were. Truth was, how the heck was I supposed to remember an off-the-cuff telepathic conversation I'd had with Allison?

"Then why do you do it?"

"I guess we did it because we can. It's easy and fast—"

"And rude."

"And rude, yes."

"But you do it anyway, even when it makes other people feel uncomfortable."

"What can I say, Mary Lou? I'm sorry. I'm learning how to be a better freak."

She looked at me, and finally unhinged her jaw,

to the great relief of her molars. She instantly looked prettier, and more relaxed. Too bad she couldn't read *that* thought.

"You're not a freak, Sam. Maybe a little inconsiderate, but not a freak."

"Remember, this is still all new to me. I hadn't known there was a telepathic etiquette."

"Well, there is. At least around me."

"Just know that I will always try to include you in the conversation, but there are going to be times when thoughts slip through, thoughts that don't always need to be vocalized."

She set her jaw, looked away. "I'm not sure how I feel about that."

"It's the best I can offer."

She didn't like it; mostly, she didn't like being left out. I scooted my stool closer to hers, and put my arm around her shoulders, similar to what Kingsley had done with me not too long ago.

I said, "I don't know why I am the way I am, or do the things I do. I don't know who makes the rules or why there are, in fact, any rules. But one such rule is that I can't communicate with family members telepathically. You're as family as it gets. It still doesn't mean I don't love you, and it doesn't mean I'm closer with Allison than I am with you. If anything, Allison annoys me to no end."

"She is kind of annoying."

"But she has a big heart," I said. "And, well, there's something special going on with her."

"Dare I ask?"

"Maybe you shouldn't."

"Okay, fine. But I still don't have to like any of this."

"Trust me, I don't like any of it either. For instance, right now I smell chicken wings and fries and beer, and they're driving me crazy."

She looked at me, and then gave me a half smile. "You're still pretending to be a vampire, huh?"

"I make a good vampire," I said.

She studied me for a moment, and then leaned her head toward mine. I did the same, and we touched heads and held hands.

"Yes, you do," she said. "Lord help me, you do."

23.

I was flying.

That was something else that I did well. Of course, I had some help in the flying department. I'd recently gone for quite an excursion. In fact, it was a trip that I would never forget, ever. And forever is a very long time for a vampire.

As I flew now, I looked up into the sky, to the crescent moon high above...and smiled. Yes, it had been quite a journey, and I had seen sights that few people would ever see.

Speaking of which, I was eager to try my newfound talent again...a talent that enabled me to go just about anywhere I wanted, at any time.

Boy, did it.

A few minutes prior to my takeoff, as I sat in

my minivan overlooking the Pacific Ocean near the Ritz Carlton in Laguna—my favorite launching point, if you will—I had studied pictures of a particular spot on earth, a spot I was certain would be cloaked in the darkness of night...but still accessible to me and only me.

I had never been to this place. In fact, I had never even been to the state.

Then again, I hadn't been to the moon either, and look at how that had turned out.

Pretty damn well, I thought. *Thank you again Talos.*

You're welcome, Sam, came a reply deep within me.

Yet another voice inside my head, I thought. Maybe all the voices were just further proof that I was crazier than a shoeshine in a shitstorm, as my grandpa used to say.

I continued flapping my wings. That such a giant, winged creature had human parents was almost laughable. But I wasn't, of course, the giant winged creature, was I?

Not quite. The creature was, in fact, a real creature who lived in a parallel universe, who used this chance to come to me, to help me, to instruct me.

To fly with me.

Are you ready, Talos, I thought.

For you, Samantha, always.

Now that just might be the sweetest thing a giant, flying bat has ever said to me.

He chuckled lightly.

I grinned inwardly, and brought up the image of the single flame, which I saw clearly in my mind's eye. The flame, which usually held either the image of Talos or me, was presently empty. Now, I summoned the image of a snowy peak located in the far, far north. Alaska to be exact. Mount McKinley, to be even more exact.

As I flew now, as the wind swept over me and I beat my great wings, I focused on the image in the flame, the snow-swept mountain peak...

And felt myself rushing toward it.

Faster and faster...

24.

I gasped and opened my eyes.

Wind buffeted me. Cold, powerful wind. So cold that even I felt its chill, although it didn't bother me much. Or, rather, it didn't bother the beast I had become. Its hide was thick and impenetrable.

Not quite, Samantha Moon. I can still be hurt, said the voice deep within me. *You would do well to remember that.*

Point taken, I thought. *Now, can I enjoy my vacation?*

As you wish.

I surveyed the landscape before me. It was a helluva landscape—and, if the creature could smile, it would be doing so now; it couldn't, so I settled for an inward smile instead.

I was high up on a frozen rocky crag. In fact, I wasn't very far from the peak itself, which was about where I had tried to "land," as I'd come to think of this last step. It was true night, and the crescent moon was farther to the south, but there it was, shining down, along with, exactly, one trillion stars, all winking at me, the flirts. I was really here. I was not in Southern California, but in the far north, far away from it all.

In a blink of an eye. I could, it seemed, go just about anywhere, including the moon. I had a thought. *Talos, could I someday return home with you?*

Not yet, Sam. You would need a visual image to hold onto. You need to see clearly where you will "land" as you put it.

But you could help me to see? I asked.

Yes, Sam. Someday.

I nodded, pleased, thrilled. That I was now high upon a forgotten crag in the dead of night, surrounded by wind and snow and the distant howl of something forlorn and forgotten, was exhilarating. I didn't belong up here. I shouldn't have been up here. But here I was. A mother of two. A private investigator, a sister, a daughter. Sitting high atop a frozen piece of rock at the far north of nowhere. Out of sight, out of mind. Alone and happy.

I didn't want to think. I didn't want to feel. I didn't want to worry. I just wanted to exist. I just wanted to *be*.

And so I sat on the rocky overhang, my great talons clinging to the rock edge, even as snow and ice began to form around them.

Ice wasn't much of a match for the great beast I had become. Neither were these extreme conditions. The beast laughed at arctic blasts of frozen air. At least, I think it did. I know I did.

Now, I tucked my wings in tight and sat high upon the world, looking down into swirling mists and billowing gusts.

And I was happy.

25.

The wonders of the Internet.

I was deemed an asset by Detective Sharp's bosses and he was given the green light to email me two weeks' worth of surveillance video in heavily encrypted, password-protected files.

A busy homicide detective didn't have time to go through two weeks' worth of surveillance tape. Hell, even a week's worth of surveillance tape, fast-forwarded, is still three or four days of mind-numbing work. Luckily, my mind didn't get numb, and my back didn't hurt, and I could sit still for hours on end without peeing or eating or drinking.

Of course, the good detective with the pointed nose and chin didn't know that.

Still, I was the best candidate for the job, and I

threw myself into it as soon as I plugged in the various passwords, and opened the files.

They were separated into days, and they had been provided by Starbucks's own security team, their loss-prevention department. Coffee was serious business, after all.

Of course, this "loss" didn't look good on Starbucks either. I knew they had been cooperative in helping the police, but there was only so much a company could do. Or anyone could do.

Hopefully, I could do a little more.

I got to it, settling in for the night.

***

The next day, I had made the kids mac n' cheese for dinner. Again. One of my four or five go-to dinners. Tonight would be Anthony's second boxing lesson with Jacky, and it had been all the boy could talk about on the drive to school, when I picked them up, and all through dinner. He had even completely forgotten to torment his sister, which was surely a sign of the impending apocalypse.

It was also a Monday night, which meant, of course, *The Voice*. Tammy ate up the bromance between Adam and Blake. And since Usher reminded me a bit of Russell, my most recent of flames, I tended to be an Usher fan. And a Shakira fan. Just loved her and her accent. With that said, there was no way in hell we were prying Tammy away from that TV. At least, not tonight. Or tomorrow, which were *The Voice* results. Damn Adam and his delicious smile. And Blake with those *ah, shucks* dimples.

Anyway, I had an hour to kill before heading out to Jacky's gym, and I killed it the best way I knew how, by plopping down in front of my computer screen and working my way through the rest of that first day of surveillance, the day Lucy Gleason had gone missing.

I was in my office, with the door closed, but I could still hear Anthony in his room, working on his footwork, breathing through his nose. He was probably quickly mastering all that Jacky had already taught him. I was prepared to watch Jacky's mind get blown tonight.

On the screen before me, the video played and customer after customer came and went. Cars came and went. Starbucks, from all appearances, appeared to be a rather profitable establishment.

As I scanned the many faces in fast-forward, Archibald Maximus's words suddenly came to me again:

"Your son's reaction to the medallion was unexpected."

"And you suspect...something else might be involved?"

"In a word, yes."

These words had been bothering me ever since they were first uttered by the ageless Librarian. What the devil did he mean? Who the hell might also be involved with my son?

I considered Jacky. My son and Jacky clearly had a bond that went beyond time, but I didn't think that was who—or what—the Librarian had been referring to.

I pushed the worry out of my mind as best as I could and went back to the video. Time slipped past, almost as fast as the people on the screen in front of me, who were depositing their hard-earned money into the bank of Starbucks in exchange for slightly burnt coffee and that Starbucks experience.

I had the video going at two times the speed, not so slow as to be real-time, but not so fast as to miss anything suspicious. Yesterday, I had started the video where I had left off with Detective Sharp. Now, it was getting past closing time, and the steady flow of customers dwindled, and then finally stopped. A few minutes later, I watched all the lights turn out. A few of the workers talked in a small huddle in the parking lot, no doubt talking about the strange day in which the lady disappeared and the cops came. And then they were gone and Starbucks was finally, mercifully dark.

"Okay, Mom, time to go!"

Only my son could sneak up on me. How he had managed to open the door without me hearing it, I didn't know. I squeaked and jumped and he grinned from the open office door.

"You have to quit doing that, Anthony."

"Doing what?" he asked, not so innocently.

"Sneaking up on me."

"But I thought you were a vampire with bat ears!" he laughed, and from down the hallway, I heard Tammy laugh, too. Great, now I was the butt of their joke.

"Just knock next time, okay?"

"Okay, sheesh!"

"Don't sheesh me."

"Shee—"

"Anthony, I'm warning you."

"Fine. Let's go already. *Please.*"

"Give me a minute. And by give me a minute, I don't mean standing in my doorway and looking at me that way."

"What way?"

"Anthony..."

"Fine."

He turned and left, but only stepped a few feet into the hallway. I could still see his shoulder. "Better?" he said.

I sighed and was just about to pause the video when I saw something interesting.

A light had turned on, from deep within the coffee shop. And, if I had to guess, it had turned on down the hallway, where the bathrooms were.

And then it turned off again.

And all was quiet.

"Mom! Jacky's waiting!"

I rolled my eyes, and shut down my computer, making a mental note to return to this spot in the video.

26.

I got a quick workout in, too.

I was fairly certain I didn't need to work out. I was fairly certain that my heightened skills just sort of "kick in" when necessary. Of course, working out made me feel normal. And feeling normal, I knew, was half the battle to fighting the demon within. Feeling human meant keeping the demon at bay for another day.

Now I worked on a punching bag at about half speed. Not too long ago, I watched Captain America in *The Avengers* send a punching bag sailing clear across the gym. Once, I'd knocked the punching bag clear off the chain, sending it tumbling a few feet. But flying across the room? Not so much. I'd leave that for the movies. I threw a final punch, sending the bag swinging, and then grabbed my towel.

I often wondered what Jacky thought of me. He, better than most, knew there was something odd about me. If being freakishly strong was odd.

And it was.

To date, I hadn't gotten very far into his thoughts, nor had I tried. I knew Jacky's own brain was muddled from years of taking hits. Punch drunk, they called it. He had brain damage, of that I knew for sure, and I thought his damage was sufficient enough for me to not gain much access.

It was just as well. Some people could keep their secrets.

Now, as I sat on the floor with my back against the wall, my towel around me, and the punching bag still swinging next to me, I watched the old Irishman work with my son, one on one, in the ring.

It was late, and so the gym was mostly empty. I checked the time on my cell. Almost closing time, in fact. Jacky had said that was okay. He was going to work with my son after hours, if it was all right with me. I told him I specialized in after hours. He gave me an odd look and shook his head. I got that a lot.

Now, as I sat and watched my son go over the footwork and handwork, I marveled again at my boy's skill. He was only ten, but he already moved with the ease and precision of a seasoned fighter. His punches were accurate, fierce, rapid-fire. I saw Jacky wincing here and there as he held up the practice mitts.

As I watched my son, as the minutes slipped past and I was almost lulled into a meditative state by the staccato sound of his punches, all punctuated by Jacky's Irish twang, a twang I never got tired of hearing, I saw something out of my peripheral vision, something that existed not quite in this world. It was standing near the gym's now-closed front door.

No, not a ghost. It was something else.

An angel.

It was Ishmael.

27.

As I approached the angel, it all started making sense to me, or some of it. Okay, maybe none of it, but I knew the angel, Ishmael, would have some answers. He'd better.

He saw me coming and glanced over at me. Then again, I suspected he knew I would come, since he had partially revealed himself to me now. He was also one of the few supernatural beings who had access to my thoughts. No surprise there, since he had once been my guardian angel.

At the door, I said to him, under my breath, "Let's talk outside."

I turned the handle and two things happened simultaneously: something snapped loudly, and Jacky was calling to me.

"The door's locked, Sam—ah, bloody hell."

"Oopsie," I said, holding up the broken handle. Yeah, I'd snapped the thing clean off. Old locks and a pissed-off vampire mama didn't go well together. "Sorry."

"You broke it," he said, staring at me from the corner of the ring. A single spotlight shone down on him and my son. Behind them, at the back of the gym, a young kid was mopping the floor. Another was wiping down the equipment. Other than that, the place was empty. That is, if you didn't count the seven-foot angel glowing next to me. And I didn't, since the others didn't seem to be able to see him, including my son. "You broke it," said the retired boxer again, this time with more awe in his voice. "Right off the goddamn door."

"I said 'oopsie.'"

"You're a freak, Sam."

"I know."

"And so is your son," he said, but as he said it, he turned and mussed Anthony's hair, and, for the moment, the Irishman forgot about his broken door handle. Anthony grinned from ear to ear, something he did far too little of.

Once outside, I tossed the broken handle aside, and told the seven-foot giant to follow me.

28.

I led him to an alley next to the gym.

"Start talking," I said, turning around, facing him. That I was ordering around my one-time guardian angel was further evidence of my descent into madness. Or further evidence that the world really is bigger and more fantastic than I'd ever dreamed possible.

"You're not mad, Sam."

"Says the seven-foot glowing angel."

"I'm here, Sam, and so are you."

"Fine, whatever. Now tell me what the devil you're doing here. And, yes, I said devil to an angel. Except, of course, we both know what kind of angel you are."

He was, of course, of the *fallen* variety.

Recently fallen, for that matter. That he had fallen because of me—or, rather, because of his misguided love for me—was a different story.

"Yes, Sam. I know what you think of me. I know you blame me for everything, but I would like to remind you that your son is in there boxing with Jacky because of what I did."

"Or didn't do," I said.

He didn't respond. My "guardian angel" had permitted me to be attacked on that fateful night eight years ago. He had looked the other way while a very old vampire had sought me out for reasons still unknown to me. Sought me out, hunted me down, take your pick. I knew now that the act wasn't random. And my guardian angel, I suspected, had played a role in it.

"I'm not as devious as you make me seem, Sam. I was aware of the interest in you."

"And you saw an opportunity."

He was beautiful. Too beautiful. Too perfect. Long, silver hair. Shoulders as wide as Kingsley's. A faint, silvery glow surrounding him. When I'd first met him, he had glowed more. His luster was wearing off, the further he dropped.

"I am not evil, Sam."

"Never said you were. But if I had to guess, you've inched a little closer to the dark side since last we spoke."

"There is no dark side, Sam. It is the same side, Sam. We are all from God. We are all one."

"Fine, whatever. Tell me, what the fuck are you

doing with my son?"

"I'm protecting him, Sam."

I nearly snorted. "What do you mean?"

"Think back, Sam. Back to when you saved your boy by turning him into something he wasn't, something immortal—"

It hit me suddenly. "He lost his own guardian angel."

"Indeed, Sam."

"But..." I wanted to refute his statement. I wanted to tell him this was all ridiculous. That guardian angels weren't real. That those were fairy tales that mothers told their children to give them comfort at night.

Except.

Except that I was standing next to such a creature. A beautiful creature, at that. And what, exactly, were guardian angels? How did they work? Who assigned them? How did they know when to protect you...and when not to protect you? Obviously, there were a lot of people getting hurt and killed in this world. Were all the guardian angels derelict in their duties?

"All good questions, Sam."

"Either someone starts answering," I said. "Or I'm going to start knocking some heads."

Ishmael gave me a rare smile. His mannerisms and gestures were...off. He was not used to holding a normal conversation. I suspected most of his existence had been spent observing humans, but rarely participating, rarely interacting. The truth was, I didn't know the extent of his abilities. He had told me he could save me from my vampirism. I wondered if that were true. There was so much I didn't know about him.

"You have lots of questions, Samantha. Perhaps we should start small."

"Perhaps you should start by telling me why you're interested in my son."

He didn't answer immediately. Not because he was gathering his thoughts, or trying to determine how much to tell me, or not tell me. No, he didn't answer me immediately because he was staring at me, through me. Deep into me.

So weird, I thought.

Finally, after an uncomfortable silence, he said, "I made an egregious mistake that night, Sam. I could have saved you. I could have directed you to go elsewhere."

"Directed me how?"

"With an impulse, with a call from a friend, with a feeling of uncertainty. I could have done something, anything, to save you from what was coming. From what I knew was waiting for you."

"But you didn't," I said, knowing the answer, of course. Knowing it all too well.

"I knew my bond would be broken with you. My covenant, if you will."

"And so you allowed me to be attacked."

"Yes, Sam. I did it—"

"I know why you did it," I said. "You've told me before. Now I want to know why other guardians for other people sit back and watch their own charges be harmed. Why? I understand you made a choice to allow me to be forever changed. But why are others doing this? Why are others allowing their humans to be harmed? Why, dammit?"

"The reasons, Samantha, are far-reaching and complicated and involve universal laws of attraction and karma, all wrapped around past lives and previous agreements."

"Agreements?"

"Yes, Sam. Believe it or not, there are some who have an agreement to kill another. Just as there are some who have an agreement to love another, or to raise another, or to help another."

"I don't believe it," I said. "I just...no, that's crazy talk."

"Perhaps, Sam. But it's true."

"Fucking nuts, if you ask me."

"I agree. But I did not create the world, Sam, or its rules. I only tried to uphold them."

"And failed miserably," I added.

He gazed at me for a long time. "Yes, Samantha. If you choose to see it that way. Yes, I failed you."

"So, I wasn't supposed to be changed that night? I had no past agreement with this vampire who changed me?"

"No, Samantha. You were to be diverted that night. I was to save you."

"Then fuck you."

He looked pained, which was a rarity for him, too. In fact, any expression of emotion was a rarity for him. Ishmael the Angel was not big on emoting. I didn't think he had much use, in fact, for expressions. Any work he'd done had been from the spiritual realm, the spiritual levels, out of sight and out of mind of mankind.

I wasn't sure where Ishmael ranked in the grand scheme of things. I wasn't sure how he filled his days and nights, where he lived, who he hung out with, or who he watched over. I didn't know if there were, say, angel bars where he knocked back some drinks with friends during their down times. I wasn't sure where in the world he lived. This world, the next world, a world in-between?

"A lot of questions, Samantha Moon," he said, reading my mind. "But just know that I am not very different from you. I am a creature of the same Source, the same God. We all are. I wasn't created to evolve. I was created to help."

"But you didn't help," I said. "At least, not me."

"No, Sam. I also wasn't created to love. Not in human terms. Not in romantic terms. But I do. I love you."

I couldn't speak. I didn't know what to say. These days, Ishmael rarely made an appearance, although I would sometimes catch him watching me from afar. That he had turned his attention to my son was news to me. But not surprisingly so. He could exist in a realm beyond even my eyes, so he could literally be anywhere.

And then it hit me like a ton of bricks.

"It's you," I said suddenly. "It's you who is giving my son his great strength."

The angel cocked his head to one side. "Yes, Sam."

"So, his strength is not from some latent..." I couldn't find the right words. I was so flabbergasted, frazzled, all the "f" words.

"The latent effect of the vampirism? No, Sam. Those effects departed the moment he was rendered back into a human. Just as his own guardian angel was released the moment he was turned into a vampire."

"Ah, fuck," I said, and found myself circling in the narrow alleyway. Fullerton isn't a big city, at least, not by big city standards. But it did have a popping downtown, and people were moving past the alley opening. Few saw me, and fewer still would see Ishmael looming over me.

I shook my hands, then ran them through my hair. Then I spun on Ishmael, and shoved him hard against the far wall. He flew back, hitting it with a physical force I wasn't expecting. The old building veritably shook.

"What did you do to my son, goddammit? What the fuck did you do to my son?"

"I gave him the edge he will need, Sam, to exist in this life without help."

"He has help from me—"

"No, Sam. Not even you can be with him at all times. Not like his true guardian angel."

"This is really, really fucked up," I said, and found myself circling the alley, shaking my hands, wanting to simultaneously smash the oversized glow stick's head into the brick wall, but needing to hear him out, too. "So, what have you done to my son? What exactly?"

"I gave him strength, Sam."

"But how?"

"I gave him some of me."

I was feeling physically ill, for the first time in a long time. "Is that why your glow has..."

"Diminished? Yes, Sam. That, and for other reasons."

I knew the other reasons, of course. I said, "So, what's going to happen to my son?"

"He will continue to have great strength, which will only increase, but not excessively so. He will, in essence, be able to take care of himself when needed."

"That's all well and dandy, but strength only goes so far."

"Your son, while not immortal, will live a long life."

"How long?"

"That remains to be seen, but longer than most."

"And what if he's..." Except I couldn't bring myself to finish the thought.

"Wounded or sick? He will heal faster than others, Sam. It will take a lot to mortally wound your son. He should be immune to most disease."

That choked me up, and I was, for the first time,

grateful to Ishmael. "Thank you," I said.
He nodded once...and disappeared.

29.

Three days later...

And I was still glued to my computer screen, watching the video feeds, hour after hour, day after day. Sometimes, I watched in real time, sometimes, at 2x the speed. I'd spent most of my free time in here, in front of my computer, and had I been mortal, my back would have been aching, my ass would have been hurt and my eyes would have been crossed.

I was none of these; mostly, I was just bored.

Except...except one thing that kept me coming back for more.

The light.

A soft, muted half-light, it still occasionally turned on in the middle of the night, often at different times and often for varying lengths. Where the light came from, I didn't know. But there it was.

There was no good reason why the light would turn on and off. My guess was, it was a smaller light deeper within the cafe. Perhaps a refrigerator light. Or a freezer light.

Two days ago, I had called the Starbucks manager and asked what type of premise security system they had. She told me she wasn't at liberty to divulge that. I almost tested whether or not I could compel her over the phone line. Instead, I called Detective Sharp and had him ask her the same question, plus a few follow-up questions. Apparently, she was at liberty to tell him. Cops get all the breaks. The Starbucks system was pretty basic. Alarm goes off if anything is broken into. No interior motion detectors. No light on timers.

Detective Sharp next wanted to know what I had found. I told him I would tell him when I knew more. He said that wasn't good enough and started to come down on me. I told him he would be the first to know as soon as I had something concrete. He didn't like it, but most cops didn't like being told what to do by private investigators. I reminded him that we were on the same team. I nearly reminded him that I was kind of cute, but luckily, he changed the subject.

"We didn't find any prints," he said.

"You checked both vents."

"Of course. They're both clean."

"She wiped them," I said. "She had the time to

clean up after herself."

"If she was there."

"It's the only thing that makes sense."

"The crime scene guys are still laughing at me," he said.

"You are kind of funny-looking."

"Look, Samantha Moon. I trusted you. You came with some good references. Hell, great references. Sherbet stands by you. And so does this Sanchez guy out of L.A. Still, I don't know you for shit, and now the guys at the station are having a good laugh at me because I had them print a fucking vent under a fucking sink at a fucking Starbucks."

"You sound annoyed."

"Damn straight I'm annoyed. Don't fuck with me, Sam. I'm going out on a fucking limb bringing you in on this, and giving you access—"

"She was in there, Detective. I promise."

"When will you show me what you have?"

"Soon."

"How soon?"

"I don't know."

"Jesus, are you always like this?"

"Sometimes," I said, "and don't call me Jesus."

30.

The kids were asleep.

I had already gone for a late-night jog, sometimes running so fast that I might as well be flying low to the ground, feeling invincible and untouchable.

I took a long shower, as hot as I could make it. One thing about taking showers in the middle of the night was that there was no one waiting in line for it. So, I used up all the hot water...and loved every second of it.

Now, dressed in a robe made of human flesh—kidding, pink terrycloth—I was back in front of my computer, prepared for an all-nighter. Of course, an all-nighter for me was really nothing more than my day job, so to speak.

Now, with my hair still wet, I curled one cold foot under me and sat at my computer, ready to dig in.

I didn't have to dig for very long.

Almost immediately, as I fast-forwarded through the fifth full day of her disappearance, after I had watched, precisely, two million people enter and exit the Starbucks in Corona, I saw something that caught my eye. And not just something.

A woman.

Exiting Starbucks.

No, not a big deal in and of itself. I had seen a million different women leave Starbucks up to this point. No, she was different. I unfurled my leg from under me and sat forward, pausing the video, capturing the woman just as she was stepping off the sidewalk that wrapped around the building.

I checked the time on the video: 1:17 pm.

I rewound the video a few seconds—hell, I'd gotten quite adept at manipulating the video controls, having spent the past three days working them—and watched her step out of the Starbucks again, this time closely watching her.

She was smallish, about the size of Lucy, if I had to guess. And I did have to guess. It was my job to guess...to make an informed guess. The woman on the screen was walking with her head down, and talking into a cell phone. The woman had black hair. Very black hair. Almost too black for her skin tone.

Interesting.

Lucy, of course, had light brown hair. The woman was also wearing different clothing, too. Shorts and a tank top. She carried a medium-sized handbag under her arm.

A different handbag than what Lucy came in with.

Maybe it wasn't her.

The woman paused briefly and actually shaded her eyes, even though she was wearing Jackie-O-type sunglasses. She paused and waved her hand. A red SUV, whose license plate was unreadable, pulled up next to the curb, and the woman with the sunglasses, with the pitch-black hair and pale skin, got into the passenger seat, and shut the door.

The SUV pulled away and was gone.

I frowned at the whole scene, replayed it twice more, and then did what any detective would do. I rewound to the early part of the day and painstaking went through each minute of the video.

And at no time did a dark-haired woman with the big sunglasses actually come into Starbucks.

She only exited.

It was Lucy; I was sure of it.

I could have kissed someone.

Even Kingsley.

31.

"So, the broad's alive," said Detective Sharp.

"Yes," I said, "And no one says the word *broad* anymore."

"Too bad. It's a good word. My pops used to say it."

It was midday, and we were in his brightly lit office. A few minutes earlier, gasping and whimpering, I had dashed across the half-empty parking lot, only to push through the heavy glass doors. Once inside, I did all I could to compose myself as quickly as possible, although I might have whimpered a little.

Now, in his too-bright office—and sitting as far away from the direct sunshine as possible—I said,

"Let me guess, your father was a cop, too."

"How'd you guess?"

"Because you sound like a cop stuck in the seventies."

"What can I say? I grew up with 'the boys,' as my father used to call his cop friends. They were over all the time."

"No mom?"

"She died young. Just me and my pops."

"He's dead, too?"

"Five years now. Ain't a day goes by that I don't miss him."

"He's here now," I said.

"Say again?"

"Your pops is here now. He's standing behind you. His hand is on your shoulder. You can probably feel a tingle there."

He reached up and made a small movement toward his shoulder, and then pulled up short. "Not cool. Who the hell sent you—"

"Shut up and listen," I said. Mercifully, his office door was closed. I hadn't expected to do a reading today, or to give a message from Spirit. I didn't have a TV show where a camera crew was following me around, waiting eagerly for me to give a stranger a reading. And I sure as hell wasn't from Long Island. But, nonetheless, I could see into the spirit world, and I think spirits took the opportunity, sometimes, to relay a message through me.

Your friendly neighborhood vampire.

I said, "I can see spirits, you big boob. I'm kind

of like a medium, only cooler."

"Wait. What—"

"Your dad is here. He's a big guy, bald. At least, that's how he's projecting himself to me right now. He's still holding your shoulder. You should be feeling a serious tingling there right about now. He's telling me, over and over, how proud he is of you."

"If this is a joke..."

"No joke, Detective," I said. In the past, I couldn't hear spirits. These days I could, especially vociferous, loud spirits. His father was such a spirit. I relayed his loving message to his son, and when I was done, Detective Jason Sharp was left sobbing at his desk, a real mess. Spirits have that kind of effect on people.

His father seemed to nod, patted his son again, and faded out slowly.

***

Detective Sharp finally looked up from all his blubbering and said, "That was so unfair."

"I don't make the rules," I said. "And your father wanted to come through."

"He's pushy like that."

"Oh, and he also wanted me to tell you not to be such a dick when you talk to me on the phone."

"Did he really—oh, bullshit. You're messing with me."

"I am."

"I guess I was a bit of a douche on the phone."

"A bit, and I hate that word."

"Sorry. Guy talk."

"If you haven't noticed yet..."

"Yeah, yeah, you're a broad."

"That I am, and like I said, no one says that word anymore."

"Well, I'm bringing it back. Now, can we get back to work?"

We did. I first showed him the various points when the muted light had turned on in the back of Starbucks, then progressed quickly over to the fifth day.

"Now watch."

"I'm watching."

When the woman with the dark hair and big sunglasses appeared on the screen, Sharp said, "Well, I'll be damned."

"That makes two of us."

"What?"

"Never mind," I said. "Any mention in the report of anyone with a red SUV?"

"No," said Sharp.

"What about her phone records?"

"She never used her phone again, neither calls nor texts after she disappeared."

"She's using a throwaway phone, then," I said.

"Would be my guess." He looked at me. "So, if we find the red SUV..."

"We find the broad," I said.

He raised an eyebrow. "Broad?"

I shrugged. "What can I say, I guess it's growing on me."

32.

It was late.

I'd spent the day debating whether or not to tell my client about his wife, and decided now was not the time. I needed more answers. And I would find them, sooner or later.

I'd also spent the day thinking about Kingsley. I didn't often spend my free time thinking about my ex-boyfriend who cheated on me, who had been manipulated to cheat on me. Kingsley had, in fact, proven himself to be a good man this past year, despite the fact that I had been treating him like shit.

He'd come through more than once, saving my ass more than once. Being there for me, through thick and thin.

I recalled his tender words, uttered to me not that long ago, as we sat in his own oversized SUV.

"The big oaf," I mumbled, shaking my head now as I sat in my office, staring down at the notes I'd made. I had a game plan to find Lucy, and it consisted of contacting anyone and everyone that Lucy had ever known. It would be a lot of work. Or, as Tammy would say, a crap-ton of work. Luckily, I was up for a lot of work.

I sighed and thought again of Kingsley and those big amber eyes of his, and that hair—Jesus, all that hair. And then it happened...for the first time in well over a year, I remembered what it had been like to run my fingers through that hair. His hair. His thick, yet soft hair.

It had been heavenly, exciting, intoxicating.

Lord help me.

I drummed my fingers on my desk, listening to the sounds of Anthony's snores, which seemed to be growing louder these days, then double-clicked on my AOL IM icon on my computer screen.

***

Hi, Fang.

Good evening, Moon Dance.

And what are you doing on this fine night? I wrote.

You might not want to know, Moon Dance.

A woman?

Yes.

Then why the heck are you IM-ing me?
She's asleep.
Is she human?
Yes.
Are you feeding from her?
I did, yes.
Is she a willing donor? I asked.
Yes.

The demon inside me perked up at this. I perked up, too, but it wasn't because of the demon. At least, I didn't think it was.

No, I thought, *it's her. She's the catalyst for all of this, remember that.*

Who's the girl? I asked.
Do you really want to know, Sam?
I wouldn't have asked otherwise.
She's an ex-girlfriend.

I knew, of course, what had happened to an earlier girlfriend of his, hell, the whole world knew. He had drained her dry in his lap while making love to her, back when he was a teenager, back when he didn't truly understand the depths of his depravity.

Does she know she's a donor? I asked.
She knows everything about me, Sam. I have no secrets from her.
So, she's willingly giving herself to you?
Yes, Sam.
Do you love her?

There was a long pause before I saw him typing again on his computer screen. Amazingly, surprisingly, I didn't feel jealous. Well, not *too* jealous. I wondered if my thoughts of Kingsley had something to with that.

Yes, I think so.

I nodded to myself and sat back and analyzed how I felt about that. Yes, there was some jealousy. I did, after all, have feelings for Fang. There was mostly confusion, though. My feelings for Fang were all over the map. He'd done much to help me in the early days, and, later, to turn my life upside down. His siding with Hanner broke my heart. In the end, he had been compelled to act by a vampire much more powerful than me, and much older, too. Still, Fang had made the decision to go behind my back, to move forward without me. And he was doing just that now, with yet *another* woman.

Yes, I was jealous, but I also felt something else.

I felt liberated.

Seeing him like this. Or, rather, hearing him describe his current situation was a reminder to me of how far we had fallen, how distant we had become. Did he still love me? I think so. Love doesn't just go away. Even a small part of me still loved Danny and missed him. A very, very small part of me, granted.

So, Fang wasn't sure about his feelings with his girlfriend. I'd let him figure that out, in his own way, and in his own time. Truth be known, what I missed most was our sweet connection via the Internet. Via the old-school AOL instant message.

Chatting with him now—even reading words

that upset me and concerned me—felt natural. It felt right. It felt like how things should feel. This past year had been one long, crazy-ass ride, and now things were finally, finally as they should be.

I typed: *Well, Fang, I hope you can figure out your feelings for her.*

I'm in no rush, Sam. She gives my life balance, security. She accepts me for who I am, exactly what I am. She doesn't judge. She only loves.

And gives you a fresh supply of blood.

Yes, Sam. There is that, too.

We were silent for a long time. His "typing" icon remained silent. Finally, I wrote: *You had the diamond medallion all along.*

You knew about that?

Yes. It looked different than the others, so I wasn't sure what it was.

I wasn't sure what it was either, truth be known.

Where did you get it?

The curiosity museum, he wrote.

Where they displayed your teeth? I wrote, referring to the teeth that now hung around his neck, looking to all the world like miniature elephant tusks. They were teeth that had been extracted from Fang long ago, in an insane asylum. Yeah, Fang was messed up, perhaps more than I might ever really know.

Yes. When I went back for my teeth, after I dispatched the owner, I saw the medallion in his safe.

So, you took it?

Of course.
And had been wearing it ever since.
Yes, Sam.
And you still have it?
No, I'm sorry.

My mouth opened and I think a sound squeaked out.

Fang continued typing: *I didn't know what I had. I didn't know its value. I just knew it was special.*

I nodded suddenly. I wrote: *But Hanner knew.*

Yes. She knew that wearing it would possibly nullify my vampirism.

And you couldn't have that, I wrote.

No, Sam.

So, you removed it?

Yes. I had to. It was the price I had to pay for her to change me. I gave it to her happily.

I nearly called him an idiot. Instead, I took a few deep breaths and sat back...and that was when it hit me.

She's still alive, isn't she?

Maybe. If she figured out how to unlock it. She was having trouble with that part.

But I saw the demon escape her when she died. The diamond medallion removes the demon.

Maybe she struck a deal with the demon within.

To keep it inside?

Yes.

Did you see her use the medallion?

I saw her try.

And then?

And then I was compelled to do what I was told, and I lost all track of the medallion.

I drummed my pointed nails on the keyboard, thinking hard. We had left Hanner down in the cavern, under the Los Angeles River, with the silver dagger still in her. Seemed safest to leave it in her. Yes, she had seemed dead. Very, very dead. But who knew?

You never went back for her? I wrote. *To revive her or help her?*

No, Sam. I've thought about it. But no.

But you loved her.

In a way, yes. But I didn't love what she did to you and your family. That was a deal breaker for me.

I thought about that long after Fang and I said our goodbyes.

Then grabbed my car keys and hit the road.

33.

"Never thought I would come back here," said Kingsley.

"That makes two of us," I said.

"Three of us," said Allison.

"Well, I didn't invite either of you," I said.

Allison snorted. "Like we would let you come here alone, Sam!"

"Like totally," said Kingsley.

"Oh, brother," I said.

We were standing outside the familiar pile of rocks that led to the secret cavern entrance under the L.A. River. It was also the middle of the night, a good time for a vampire, a witch and a werewolf to go grave-robbing. Anyway, from all indications, the rocks hadn't been touched or moved since we had been here last, three months ago.

Now, with a cool wind blowing and the sounds of smaller animals moving in the thick underbrush nearby, Allison's words appeared in my mind: *Are we sure we want to do this, Sam?*

I caught the image in her mind...and it was of Danny's grave, which I had helped dig with my own hands, also located here in this strangest of tombs, in the woods not far from downtown Los Angeles, along the east side of Griffith Park. If anything, we were closest to the L.A. Zoo, which just so happened to be the setting to a zombie series Tammy was reading, written by a guy who wrote his own vampire series starring an undead mama not too dissimilar from me. Maybe I should sue the bastard.

Or feast on him.

Anyway, L.A. wasn't all stars, glitz and freeways. This park was proof. It was a park that housed not only the zoo, but the Griffith Park Observatory, the Hollywood Sign, and the Greek Theater. Most of which had found their ways into the movies. No surprise there, since they were just a hop, skip and a jump from Hollywood.

"I'm fine," I said aloud. "Really."

Kingsley snapped his big head around in my direction. "What? Never mind. You two are doing your telepathy thing again."

"You can't read minds?"

"No, Sam. At least, I don't think so."

"If you want," said Allison, "you can practice

with me. I'm really, really good at mind reading."

Kingsley raised his eyebrows. "Er, thanks, Allie. I'll keep that in mind."

It was no secret that my new best friend had the hots for my old boyfriend. What my new best friend didn't know—and I'd been doing my damned best to shield these thoughts from her—was that I had been thinking a lot about Kingsley these days.

Perhaps too much.

Definitely more than I should have.

Allison had every right to flirt with Kingsley, although I had made it known that it was technically still weird for me. Still, she had been polite about it, never too overt, and so far, Kingsley hadn't seemed very interested.

I suspected I knew why.

He's still in love with me, I thought, making sure my mind was sealed nice and tight. I had no reason to keep these thoughts from Allison, other than I just wanted to analyze them without prejudice or judgment or outside interference. Mostly, I wanted to understand them...and be sure of how I felt.

I looked again at the hulking man standing beside me. He had one giant boot up on a boulder. The boot wasn't a cowboy boot. It looked Italian, and expensive. It also looked good on him. He was waiting for me. They both were.

Now, of course, was not the time to analyze my feelings about Kingsley.

I nodded. "Let's do this."

Kingsley grinned, reached down with one hand, and ripped free a boulder that was much heavier than he made it look. It crashed to the ground below, making an ungodly loud thud.

He pulled free another, then another, removing them with frightening ease and speed. I almost jumped in to help, but Kingsley needed no help.

In a matter of minutes, there appeared a dark hole.

"Ladies first," he said, and stepped aside.

"Gee, thanks," I said, and led the way down.

34.

The tunnel was longer than I remembered it.

I didn't need light, nor did Kingsley, but Allison wasn't so lucky. She was also more than capable of creating her own light, which she did by creating a liquid ball of glowing plasma between her palms. At least, that was what it looked like to my eyes. I watched it grow bigger and bigger, marveling at my friend's newfound witchy talents. Then she released it into the air above us, and it followed ahead of us, a hovering, glowing, seemingly sentient ball of weirdness.

Although not necessary, the light was welcoming. As we walked, I used a trick of my own, and focused my inner eye on our immediate surroundings; in particular, what was waiting ahead of us.

It wasn't much, and the macabre scene was exactly as we'd left it.

"It seems we're alone in here," said Kingsley, and I wondered if he had somehow known I had just mentally scouted ahead.

I nodded. "From what I can see, yes."

He pointed to his ears. "From what I can hear, too."

Ah, yes. Kingsley, of course, had a skill set of his own.

Shortly, we stepped into the first of two massive, underground caverns.

***

That such a rock formation existed under L.A. was enough for me to question my sanity all over again.

But here it was.

As we stood in it, the memories began flooding back. I'm sure I wasn't the only one. We had all had a traumatic experience in here a few months ago, from my ex-husband Danny being stabbed, to Kingsley in the fight of his life, to Allison keeping two crossbow-wielding guards at bay using more of her considerable magic.

Three freaks, I thought, and strode out into the center of the first of the two caverns.

There, in the far corner, was a pile of withering bones poking through darker robes and nicer shoes. That his head was nowhere near his body was a testament to Kingsley's ferocity.

The death of that vampire had freed Fang from his own compulsion. Fang had immediately acted to stop Hanner, by plunging a silver dagger deep into her heart.

Except, of course, I hadn't been aware that she was wearing the diamond medallion at the time.

"So, what does that mean, exactly?" asked Allison, mostly following my train of thoughts.

"Means she might be alive."

"Alive how?"

"I don't know."

"It's always fun," said Kingsley, striding into the next room, "to catch only half of your conversations."

I didn't immediately follow him through stone archway and into the second cavern; instead, I paused and took a deep breath and prepared myself for what I expected to see.

After all, it was within this second cavern that we had buried my ex-husband, Danny.

After I took a moment, Allison and I entered the second cavern, and I immediately saw the reason why I hadn't seen Danny's spirit since his death. There he was, sitting next to his grave, legs crossed and looking miserable, haunting the crap out of this place. He drifted slightly, bobbing and rising, as if he were sitting on an inner tube in the shallow end of a dark pool.

He looked up as I entered.

35.

Danny is a recent spirit.

He'd been killed only months earlier, which meant I could still see a lot of his detail, even though his "light body" was composed of tens of thousands, if not millions, of tiny light particles.

"Guys, give me a minute," I said.

Kingsley looked toward the dirt pile where my ex-husband's corpse was still rotting away. He nodded, understanding. Whether or not he knew that I saw Danny's spirit, I didn't know, but he understood enough and said, "I'll go check on our friend Hanner."

Allison gave me an encouraging smile. She, too, could sometimes see into the spirit world, and I knew she, too, sensed Danny's presence. *Good luck, Sam,* she thought to me.

Thanks, I responded, and headed over to my dead ex-husband, whose spirit was looking miserable.

***

"Hi, Danny," I said, addressing the spirit.

I sat on a rock very near to where he was standing. He watched me silently, his body forming and reforming, pulsing and shimmering. Truly the body electric.

"Have a seat, Danny," I said, and patted the rock next to me. "Let's talk."

He studied me silently, rising and falling ever so slightly, drifting on currents unseen and unfelt by the living. Or even the non-living. The details of Danny's energetic body were so sharp that I could still see the mortal wound in his chest where the knife had plunged deep. I could also see the belt loops to his jeans, his shoelaces and the collar of his short. I knew, with time, such details would fade away. But for now, they were clear enough.

Unfortunately, his facial expressions were lost to me, although I could see the general outline of what had been a handsome face. I saw his ears, his mussed hair, his straight jawline. I couldn't see his eyes, and that saddened me. Danny had beautiful blue eyes.

Unsure of himself—at least, that was the impression I got—he sat next to me. If I were a new ghost, I would sure as hell be unsure of myself, too. As he sat, some of his light fragments scattered towards me like a bag of marbles that had burst. Unlike marbles, these particles of living energy moved over my right arm and around my wrist and fingers and hand before disappearing. I shivered and the goose bumps bumped.

"I should have checked on you sooner, Danny," I began. "I should have suspected you would still be down here."

He cocked his head slightly.

"I should have known you would be confused and unable to move on."

Now he cocked his head to the other side. I had his attention. I wondered how much he was really hearing, and how much he was actually comprehending.

That was when tears came, and they came hard, as I realized again that the man I had planned my future with and built a family with and had wanted to grow old with, had been forgotten in this shitty, desolate hellhole.

"I was taking care of the kids," I said, doing my best to speak through the tears. "They've been so upset."

I wanted to reach out and take his hand. And just as the thought crossed my mind, Danny did just that: he reached out with his own pulsating, crackling hand...and took my own. And he didn't stop there, he leaned over and gave me the most electrifying hug I'd ever had.

***

This was the first time I had really cried for Danny, and I did it now, in the presence of his confused ghost, at the bottom of a forgotten hole in the ground, in the place of his murder. He continued holding me, and I leaned my head in his direction, although I mostly hit air. Mostly.

"The kids miss you, but they are okay. They are both healing, but it will take time, maybe forever. I was worried about Anthony, but he has found...a new friend."

I purposely didn't mention that this was all because of Danny's idiocy. His desire to destroy me, in the end, had directly led to his death. He had aligned himself with the wrong people, people who used him.

I glanced over at Kingsley and Allison, who were both standing over another form, a form we had not bothered to bury, a form that, because of the contours of the cavern floor, I couldn't quite see.

A form who might not be dead, after all.

I knew Danny was sorry. I also knew that he was doing something that he had never done while living...sensing my thoughts. It took him dying before the idiot and I finally became truly connected.

"You're sorry," I said. "I know. I can feel it."

He nodded once, although the gesture seemed strange to him. He tried it again, liked it, and then nodded again and again.

"Okay, goofball. So you can nod. Big deal."

I might have seen the corners of his mouth rise slightly. Back in the day, before his fear of me and his love for other women, Danny had had a nice sense of humor. It was why I had married him. That, and I wanted his last name.

Now, Danny threw his head back and I saw his shoulders shake. He was laughing, and a scattered remnant of his thought appeared in my thoughts: he'd always suspected that was why I had married him.

I laughed, too, and when we were both done and had settled down, I next felt Danny's sadness.

"You miss them," I said.

He nodded his head again, and I saw something next that I didn't think I would ever soon forget: a shiny, fiery tear appeared in the corner of Danny's right eye. It slid down his face, leaving behind a blazing trail of quicksilver. The tear dropped free, and, while falling, exploded into a thousand tiny fragments of light.

"You can visit them, you know," I said. "But you can't visit them if you're stuck in here."

He cocked his head again, his way of telling me he was listening. Danny, who had always been the practical, skeptical lawyer, had found himself ill-equipped in the bewildering world of spirits.

"There's a tunnel, Danny. A tunnel of light. I know you've seen it. It will show itself every now and then. Do not be afraid of it. Go to it. Others will be waiting for you. Others you have loved, grandparents, friends, relatives. They will guide you, Danny. Go to them. Go to the light."

He looked down, and I sensed his fear.

"Do not fear it, Danny. Go to it. Only then will you be able to leave this place...and see your kids again."

He turned and stared at me some more, silently, rising and falling in that realm between worlds, layered over this world.

"I have work to do, Danny."

He nodded and released my hand. But before he did so, he thanked me as best as he could. Through feelings, and a hint of thought.

"We'll get you out of here, Danny boy," I said. "And maybe we'll see you around sometime?"

He might have smiled at that.

36.

There she was.

We all stared down at what had once been a very old and very powerful vampire. No, not one of the oldest, but certainly she'd had her fill of human blood over the centuries.

"This medallion..." began Kingsley.

"The diamond medallion," I said.

"Yes, this diamond medallion...it's different than the other medallions, no?"

I nodded and, staring down at a woman I had also once called a friend, I told Kingsley what I knew: the diamond medallion vanquished the demon from within, all while allowing the owner to retain all the vampiric power, with none of the ill side effects. That she was dead, there was no doubt.

Her skin had dried around her skull, knuckles and wrists. The skin itself was just months from rotting off completely.

"Would you remain immortal?" asked Kingsley, unaffected by the gruesome sight before us. Truth was, I was unaffected, too. Death wasn't something to fear...but something to embrace.

You're scaring me, Sam, came Allison's words.

I ignored her, and said to Kingsley, "my understanding is, yes. Or something very close to it. With the diamond medallion, you get to pick and choose the gifts you want."

"Sweet deal. Wish I had that," said Kingsley. "How do we know that Hanner didn't use the medallion, and, you know, use up its juice?"

"For one, she's dead. Two, I saw the demon leave her when she was killed."

"So, she hadn't figured out how to use it?"

I stared down at her grinning skull. Her eyes had rotted out. "My guess, is no."

"So, what do we do now, Sam?" asked Allison.

I knelt down and said, "For starters, we check her out."

I tore open her blouse, revealing a bloody, mostly empty bra. The silver tip of the knife protruded exactly where her heart would have been. Fang had been deadly accurate.

Allison made a noise and looked away. I didn't blame her. The scene before us was horrific and macabre, the stuff of nightmares. I loved it. Loved it more than I should have. I stared down at the ghoul before me, intrigued, excited.

Stop, Sam. Just stop, came Allison's voice.

She's weak, said a voice deep, deep within me, too deep for even Allison to hear.

I ignored them both and said, "No medallion."

"So, what next?" asked Kingsley.

I shrugged. "Let's check her pockets."

Her clothes were decidedly looser on her than they had been a few months ago. As I searched her, I wondered where her own soul had gone, and if she had finally reconnected with her dead son. Or, worse, had her soul dissipated into nothingness?

No, I thought, as I moved over to her other side, careful of the knife blade projected through her chest. *I can't accept that. Souls are eternal. Even more so than vampires.*

I knew some believed that a vampire was, in fact, *all soul*. You kill the vampire, you kill the soul, too.

Don't worry about that now, Sam, came Allison's reassuring thoughts. *You're not dying any time soon.*

Thank you, I said, and reached down into Hanner's front pocket. And there it was.

I pulled it out by its leather strap and held it up. It was smaller than the other medallions...and contained only a single diamond rose in the center, which glistened brilliantly in Allison's ball of magical light.

I half expected to hear Fang's voice at this moment. I half expected this to be an elaborate trap.

I half expected for other vampires—or even vampire hunters—to descend upon us.

But none of that happened. Real life wasn't the movies, of course. This wasn't an episode of *The Vampire Diaries*. Real life didn't throw every conceivable, nonsensical twist and turn at you.

At least, not this time.

I held up the medallion before me, letting it spin and catch the light.

For the first time in a long time, I felt hope.

37.

I was back in the Occult Reading Room.

Archibald Maximus greeted me, and then asked me to wait while he disappeared into the back rooms. What was back there, I didn't know, and what he did back there, I didn't know that either.

The Occult Reading Room wasn't very big. It was located on the third floor of the main Cal State Fullerton Library. The room itself was found against the far wall, which took some time getting to, since the floor itself was nothing short of epic, with rows upon rows of books as far as the eye could see. Once you reached the far wall, there it was, through a nondescript doorway that existed for some, but not for others. If you needed the room, it was there. If you were *ready* for the room, it was there. If not, then you were shit out of luck.

"Let those with eyes see," said Archibald, as he approached me now down the short hallway behind the help desk, a hallway I had never been down. "Let those with ears hear." He stopped behind the desk and smiled. "Do you understand, Sam?"

"I do," I said. "And I think someone is a little full of himself."

The Librarian threw his head back and laughed. "It does sound a bit pretentious, doesn't it? But it's a truth, Sam. A universal truth, in fact." He motioned to the array of books shelved neatly throughout the room. "Most of this information would be lost on those not ready."

"It would be lost on me," I said. "Yet, I'm here."

"You are further along than you might know, Sam."

"Further along in what?"

"To understand the mystery of it all."

"And you understand?" I asked.

"No, Sam. But that is the goal, is it not?"

"If you say so. I just want to be a good person, a good mom. I don't want to kill or be intrigued by death. It's not me. It's *her*."

"Understandable, Sam. I think you will get there. But, yes, you are not my typical seeker."

"And who is your typical seeker?"

"An initiate well-versed in the occult, well-versed in mastering himself inside and outside, and mastering those around him as well."

"And then, they come to you for what?"

"Their final training, if you will."

"Pardon my French, but who the fuck *are* you?"

"It's not French, Sam. And I have been many people, throughout time and space."

"Anyone I would know?"

"I doubt it, Sam."

"But you are an alchemist," I said.

"I am that, and much more."

"Lucky you," I said. I drummed my fingers on the desk, thinking. "I've heard of Hermes. And Thoth. Actually, I've heard of the *Book of Thoth*. I couldn't tell you what it is, or what's in it, but I've heard of it, somewhere."

"Many people have, although few understand it."

"Oh, God, please tell me you didn't write it. And if you did, can I get it on my Kindle?"

He smiled. "Hermes was my teacher, Sam. Hermes Trismegistus, to be exact. The Thrice Great."

"Okay, now you're just making up words."

"Master Hermes would have smiled at your flippancy, and perhaps added a joke of his own. He had a great sense of humor."

"Had? So, he's dead now?"

"He's moved on."

"Of course," I said. "No one dies anymore. So, who was he?"

"The father of alchemy, and my teacher."

"You sound like you miss him."

"Every day, Sam."

"You knew him for a long time," I said, sensing the depth of their relationship.

"Centuries."

I think I hit upon a nerve, and he changed the subject. "You have brought something with you?"

"Would be more impressive," I said, "if you couldn't read my mind." I slipped my hand inside my sweater pocket and removed the smooth, dense object. I placed it before him on the help desk. "This look familiar?"

"It does."

"I took it from the corpse of a vampire."

"Sounds like the beginning of a novel."

"Or the end," I said.

He motioned toward it. "May I?"

"Be my guest. You created the damn thing."

He smiled and picked up the glittering relic, turned it over in his hand, and rubbed his thumb across the back. *Did he just activate it?* I wondered.

"A smudge," he said, grinning.

He continued turning it and polishing it, almost affectionately.

"Yes, affectionately, Sam. It took many, many decades to perfect this very relic."

"And yet, you let it collect dust in a curiosity museum for God knows how long—"

"Thirteen years. And I'm not God, although we are all aspects of God."

I opened my mouth to speak, closed it again.

"I'm always aware of my creations, Sam. I am

deeply connected to them, you see."

"Actually, I don't see, but I'll take your word for it. I still don't understand how you could let something so valuable out of your sight."

"Never out of my inner sight, Sam."

"Enough with the doublespeak, Max," I said. "You know what I mean."

"I do, and there comes a time when every parent must release his children into the world. You will discover this soon enough."

"I'd prefer to not think about it."

He smiled. "You are equipping your children marvelously, Sam."

"And you know this, how?"

"Your children are always at the forefront of your mind, Samantha. I do not have to plumb very deep to see what a remarkable job you are doing, under the circumstances. A mother's love is a beautiful thing."

"Let's stop right there on a high note, before you start creeping me out."

"Agreed," he said. "Back to the medallion. It needed to find its way into the world—"

"Yes, yes, like children. I got that. But why?"

"Don't you know, Sam?"

"Know what?"

"So that it could find *you*. On its own."

I looked at him; he looked at me. Somewhere behind me, a student walked past the Occult Reading Room without missing a step. *Let those with eyes see,* and all that jibber-jabber.

"You could have just given it to me, you know," I said. "And saved yourself a lot of time."

"And what fun would that have been?" His eyes might have twinkled. "But that's not the way it works, Sam. I did not know it was for you, for starters. Not until I met you. Not until you started gathering the other medallions."

"Then you're not surprised that I have this one, too?"

"No, Sam. I would have been surprised if your one-time friend Detective Hanner had figured out how to unlock it."

"But she couldn't?"

"No. But she tried valiantly."

"I take it there's more to it than just wearing it?"

"A tad more."

I drummed my freakishly long nails on his help desk, a desk that looked like any other help desk at any other library. The room looked normal, too. Only the oversized, ancient-looking books that filled the nearby shelves looked anything but normal. They looked dark, felt dark and *were* dark. Some darker than others.

"Why me?" I asked suddenly. "Why am I the one finding all these medallions? Why do you help me? I'm just me, no one. Just a mom who got attacked a long time ago."

As I spoke, I couldn't help but notice the Librarian's demeanor softening. He set the medallion down on the desk, near my drumming fingers. He inhaled and, for the first time ever, I saw the young man who wasn't young express real emotions. And the emotion was heartbreak.

I looked at the medallion, and then, looked him in the eyes. No, I couldn't read his mind, but I sensed there was something big going on here.

Sensed it from deep within me.

Sensed it from *her*, in fact. The demon within.

A cold shiver ran up and down my spine. "The demon inside me..." I began, but I was unable to find the words. Not with Archibald looking at me like that, with so much emotion that it was breaking my heart for reasons I didn't know.

"She wasn't always a demon," he finished. "She was my mother once."

38.

Maximus let me have these moments to work out what I had just heard, except I wasn't doing a very good job of it.

"I think I need to sit," I said.

I found one of the plush reading chairs that were scattered throughout the room. Of course, I'd never actually seen anyone reading in the chairs, but that was par for the course. I wasn't sure who the Librarian's other clients were, or initiates, as he put it. Truthfully, I didn't want to know, either.

I sat; he took the chair across from me.

"Just two normal people sitting at the library," I said, "although I'm probably talking a little loudly."

"No one can hear you, Sam."

"Of course not. Why should they?"

"Sam, you're upset."

"Wouldn't you be?"

"I can see how I wasn't forthright—"

"How long have you known that the bi—the thing inside me was your mother?"

"You can say bitch, Samantha. My mother is very much one, and far worse, truth be told."

"So, now the truth is being told?"

"Sam, remember that part where I said let those with ears hear—"

"Well, I have ears, and you damn well could have told me sooner."

"I didn't know, Sam, not until you arrived with the diamond medallion. Then I knew for sure—"

"But you suspected all along?"

"I did, yes. The medallions would seek her out. I would know if it was her only if—and only if—all four medallions were returned back to me."

"By the same person," I said.

"Yes."

"You could have told me..."

"No, Sam. I could not. It would have affected the outcome. I needed to know, and I needed to know organically."

His words made sense, although, for me, one demon was the same as any other. Mother or not, I wanted her out. But even that thought was so...fantastical that I was having trouble wrapping my brain around it. I said as much, although I knew that Maximus was closely following my every thought.

He answered with, "Every highly evolved dark

master started as a human, Sam. And every alchemist, too. Your angel friend is the exception. He was never human."

"You know about him, huh?"

"I'm afraid I do, but he is for another discussion at another time."

"Fine," I said. "Let's get back to your mother."

"She came from a long line of mystics, which shouldn't come as a surprise."

"Right," I said. "Seeing how you turned out."

He nodded. He was sitting forward now in the chair, elbows on his knees. He looked like any other college student. He was handsome, youngish, and clean shaven of the previous pointy beard he had once worn. The deep intelligence and kindness in his eyes gave him away. I noticed that at various times when I had previously seen him, his eyes appeared bright blue, or violet, or even bright green. Today, they were bright blue again and I chalked it up to some mysterious alchemy of his old soul. He was clearly not like other students. Or like anyone else, for that matter.

"My mother was seduced by the darkness, to put it lightly. She wasn't, shall we say, very disciplined."

"She looked for shortcuts," I said.

He nodded. "Very good."

"What year are we talking about?"

"Fourteen thirty-two. Over six and a half centuries ago."

"Gee, you don't look a day over two hundred."

He cracked a smile. "There are far older in the world, Sam. I'm a relative newbie to all of this."

"Did you just say 'newbie'?"

"I did, and I'm proud of it. It's a good word."

I wanted to laugh at the insanity of it all, but that would have only added to the insanity. I kept my emotions in check and said, "So, your mother took shortcuts."

"They all took shortcuts, Sam. They sought immortality quickly, without the necessary work."

"And you put in the necessary work?"

"I did."

"With Hermes?"

"Yes. Myself and others."

"Other alchemists?"

"Yes, there are many out there like me."

"Many?"

"Okay, a few."

"So, your mother and others like her, they sought a shortcut to immortality?"

He nodded. "And their shortcut was a very dark and wicked one. They hurt a lot of people. They hurt themselves, too."

"They hurt you?"

"Yes, Sam. I was witness to many horrible acts. It is why I sought another purpose."

"To stop her."

"To stop *them*. But I needed help."

"Hermes?" I said.

"Yes, Sam. The greatest of us all. The master's master, as he is referred to."

"Sounds kind of badass."

"The baddest of all asses."

Okay, now I did snort. "So, what did Hermes do?"

"He removed them, Sam."

"All of them?"

"Yes. And it wasn't easy. There were battles and wars, often fought outside of history books. My mother and others like her—that is, those who mastered the dark arts—put up a tremendous battle. We lost some good people, and so did they. But in the end..."

"Good triumphed," I said.

"In a word, yes."

"And how long did that last?"

"Perhaps a half century."

I did the math, and saw the date in my mind. "That would be the end of the fourteen hundreds."

"Correct, Sam."

"Don't say it," I said, suddenly gasping.

"Yes, Sam. There was a warlord king in those days. A powerful and wicked young man who delighted in killing others. Who delighted in impaling them and watching them bleed."

"Don't say it," I said again.

"Yes, Sam. Dracula was the first of your kind."

"Damn, you said it."

39.

"Is Dracula still alive today?"

"Yes, Sam."

"And the old vampire, Dominique, the one who Kingsley killed in the cavern—"

"Was one of the first to be turned by Dracula."

"Am I dreaming?" I asked.

"No, Sam."

"That's exactly what I would expect someone in my dream to say."

"I assure you, Samantha. This is all very real, and it's happening now."

"Fine," I said, sitting back. "Continue."

And continue he did. The dark masters had found a way to circumvent Hermes' spell that had cast them from this world. And the way back in was through *possession*.

"Okay, that part I know," I said, "but where does your mother fit into all of this?"

"She was one of the greatest of her kind."

"Dark masters?"

"Yes," said Maximus. "I watched her kill many and destroy many lives. I watched her torture and maim and wreak havoc. I watched her drink blood from the very old and the very young."

"Was she a vampire then?"

"There were no vampires then."

"Okay, now that's just sick."

"That was Mother."

"No wonder you have issues."

He smiled sadly, and continued, "She was unusually powerful. Unusually proficient in the darker arts. She didn't have to go this route, you know. She could have done goodness in the world."

"Maybe your mother was a good, old-fashioned psychopath."

"I suspect so."

"Lucky me," I said.

"Quite the opposite, Sam. Lucky her."

"What does that mean?"

"I suspect she is benefiting by being a part of your life, Sam."

"I don't understand."

"She is with you constantly, seeing through your eyes, experiencing life through you."

"Yeah, so? She's a parasite."

"You are her first host, Sam."

"Do you have any idea how creepy that sounds?"

"I imagine, but hear me out. She has been waiting for the right person for many centuries."

"And I'm the right person?"

"Yes."

"Why?"

"I'll explain that in a moment."

"How about if you explain it now?"

"Very well, Sam. You are particularly attractive to her because of your bloodline."

"What about my bloodline?" I had a very bad feeling about this.

He held up his hand. "No, Sam. You are not my distant relative, but you are a distant relative to someone else."

"Oh, God. Please don't say Dracula."

"Not Dracula, Sam."

"Then who—" Then it hit me. "Hermes."

"Yes, Sam. The greatest alchemist who'd ever lived had a child."

I thought back to the time in the cavern. Hanner had said my sister would do just as well. They were prepared to kill me and infect her with the same demon who lived in me, his mother. And my sister would have come from the same bloodline, of course.

"Now that you know, Sam, perhaps you can understand why your own powers seem to be growing so quickly. Combine your lineage with my mother's power...and you have the potential to be unstoppable."

"I don't want to be unstoppable. I just want to be me."

"I know, Sam."

"So, what do I do?" I asked. "Remove her?"

"You could."

I ran my fingers through my hair. "Then what would stop her from going after my sister? Or my daughter?"

"Good points, Sam."

"What does she want with me, anyway?"

"Only an offspring of Hermes can unseal the doorway between worlds."

"Okay, now I know I'm on the set of *The Vampire Diaries*." I looked around. "Where's Damon? Hell, I'll even take Stefan."

"This is not a film set, Sam. I'm sorry."

I sat back, exhaled. "Let me guess: if she can possess me completely, she could potentially return all the banned dark masters?"

"Yes, Sam."

"Well, fuck." I stood and paced along the carpeted area before the reading chairs. Maximus sat back, fingers steepled under his chin, watching me. "I almost..." and I couldn't believe I was about to say this, "I almost think I *shouldn't* release her. That I should keep her caged in me. That I should keep fighting her."

He said nothing, watching me carefully.

I continued pacing. "I am doing a good job of fighting her. But...but she's gaining ground. I can

feel her inching closer to the surface."
    "You can fight her, Sam."
    "Fight her how?"
    "You won't believe me if I say it."
    I stopped in front of him. "Try me."
    "You fight her with love."

40.

"She's laughing," I said.

"I imagine she is. My mother rarely, if ever, used words like *love*."

"She's calling you worthless, a disappointment. Should I stop?"

Maximus shook his bowed head. I couldn't see his expression, but from what I could tell, this was nothing he hadn't heard before. "Better to let it out, Sam, than to keep her vitriol bottled up inside you."

"She says you're an embarrassment. She's telling me that you are my enemy, to not listen to you, to fight you. To kill you."

"Nice chatting with you, too, Ma," he said.

The demon inside—his mother—was filling my thoughts with her anger, her rage. They bubbled up from down deep. I sensed I could have stopped them. Demanded that she back off. I sensed she would have to listen, too. That she *had* to listen. But I spoke her words anyway.

"She wants to make a deal with me. If I give her a few minutes a day, or a week, she will back off, leave me alone."

"I caution you against it—"

"She tells me I will have peace again, if I give her a chance to make an occasional appearance."

"Sam, please..."

"She tells me that it won't hurt, and that she won't hurt any of my loved ones."

"Sam..."

"She's telling me that she and I, together, could start something new, something great. We could stand up to you, and to the world, and create our own destiny."

"Sam, I beg you..."

"Well, don't worry. I told her to go fuck herself and crawl back under the rock she came from."

The Librarian, who was leaning forward on his elbows and staring at me with enough intensity to power a Prius, exhaled audibly. "Thank you, Sam."

"I'm not sure what's going on, or how she intends to use me, or what she intends to do with me once she has me, but one thing I do know: she's pure evil."

"That's my ma."

"So, what's this business about beating her with love?"

"It's happening already."

"What's happening now?"

"You. You are effecting change just by being who you are. She is forced to see love, to see good, and she hates it. It's why she is pushing to get out. Your life is affecting her."

"My life is chaotic," I said. "My life is filled with my kids fighting and Anthony's skid marks. And not necessarily in that order."

He smiled. "Perhaps, Sam. But it's also filled with love. You loving your kids. You sacrificing for your kids. You loving and caring for your friends and family. She cannot help but to feel it as well. And this is a new experience for her. The more you love, the more your spirit shines, and the more she is affected."

"And then what?" I said.

"And then, I don't know."

"You expect her to change?"

"Love has that effect on people. It's been known to happen. Love and hate are but two ends of the same pole. Extreme ends, granted. But each day you love is another day she is being exposed to such influences."

"And another day that she rebels," I said.

"Indeed, Sam. I did not say it would be easy."

"So, I'm a big experiment."

"You don't have to be, Sam."

"No," I said. "Except, if I let her loose with the diamond medallion, she might go after my family next. To conveniently arrange for one of them to be attacked, too."

"I would not put it past her."

"So, I'm stuck with her."

"That is up to you, Sam."

A horrible thought just occurred to me. "What's to stop other dark masters—not necessarily your mother—from attacking my daughter and sister, since we are all descendants of Hermes, as you say."

"It's a good question. My mother was clearly one of the strongest, greatest of her kind. It could only be her, or someone like her, who could perform the necessary magicks to bring down the veil."

"So, how many are like her?"

"Only a small handful, Sam. Three or four at most. And these are currently in residence with other hosts."

"You mean they're currently vampires."

"And werewolves, too."

"Demons and vampires and werewolves, oh my!" I said.

I paused next to the diamond medallion, picked it up and turned it over in my hand. It caught the surrounding light, and returned it a thousand times. Pure gold and the clearest diamonds will do that. "I need to get a drink," I said.

"I bet. I could use a stiff one myself."

"Stiff one? Yeah, you are an old-timer," I said.

"Well, Sam. What would you like to do with the medallion?"

"I want you to hold onto it," I said. "For now. I might someday come back for it and take my chances."

"Fair enough." I handed it over to him and he took it from me. He stood and slipped it into his pants pocket, and went around the help desk, where I was used to seeing him.

"I guess I'm doomed to drink blood for all eternity," I said. "And stay out of the light of the sun."

The Librarian snapped his fingers. "About that. I've been a busy boy back here." He motioned to the hallway behind him.

"I take it those aren't just offices back there."

"Far from it."

"A lab?" I asked. I had an image of frothy test tubes and beakers and Bunsen burners.

He grinned. "Something like that. Hold on."

I held onto the desk, shaking my head over the craziness of it all. I checked the time on my cell. *Shit! I was late picking up the kids again.* Damn the Librarian and his crazy hours. I sent Tammy a quick text and told them to wait for me, and that I was on my way. Her text came back just as the Librarian returned. Her text read: *Get a grip, Mom!*

Never had truer words been spoken. Or texted.

"Is texted a word?" I asked.

"It is now," he said, and stepped behind the help desk again. He held out two fists. "Pick a hand."

"A game?" I asked.

"Games are good for the soul. Pick one."

I picked the right. He turned his fist over and opened it. There. Sitting in the center of his palm, was one of the prettiest gold rings I'd ever seen. Embedded within it was a blue sapphire that sparkled, amazingly, as bright or brighter than the diamond medallion.

"Beautiful!" I said. "Is that for me?"

"Yes, Sam. Put it on."

I did, on my right index finger. It fit perfectly. "Don't look so smug," I told him. "You got my ring size from my mind."

He looked satisfied anyway. "Pick again."

"More games?" I asked.

His eyes twinkled for an answer.

I touched his left fist, and he opened it, revealing another ring, with a slightly different design. This one contained an opal. I said, "What are these?" And then it hit me. "They're from the earlier medallions."

"Indeed, Sam."

"But...I destroyed them."

"In a way, yes, but I managed to rebuild them. Remember, I am the one who created them." He pointed to the first ring. "The sapphire ring will enable you to exist comfortably in the sunlight. You experienced that before, when you wore it as a medallion. Remember, you are still not at full strength in the sunlight, but at least you will not suffer. The opal ring will allow you to—"

I couldn't contain myself. "To eat!" I screamed "And to drink!"

"And to be merry. Yes, Sam."

"Holy shit! I could kiss you." And I did just that, planting a kiss on his cheek. "But you warned against having all four medallions together. That a dark master could use them to release one of his kind."

"Indeed, Sam. As you can see, these aren't medallions. That error has now been fixed."

"I could kiss you again," I said. "And again and again."

And I did so, again and again. Showering the young man who wasn't really young with kisses on his cheeks and forehead.

41.

It had been a week, and I was waiting.

The downside of working as a private investigator from one's home was that all sorts of sketchy types could turn up. Which was why I rarely gave away my home address to anyone I hadn't screened first. Without a published address, I was hard to find. That was a good thing...unless you *wanted* to be found.

And this time, I very much wanted to be found.

Which was why I was using another detective's office. Mr. Jim Knighthorse was a piece of work, and his office was riddled with bullet holes, bloodstains and dog hair, but he let me borrow it for the week, and for that, I was grateful.

Presently, he was on a road trip to Sedona,

following up clues to his own case, one that involved a child actor who might or might not be dead. Private eyes are like that. We follow the clues to wherever they may take us. Sometimes they take us to dark places. Other times, they take us to Sedona. At least, he got to write-off a trip.

Anyway, using Knighthorse's office as a launching point, I followed up with anyone and everyone who might know Lucy Gleason. I visited her parents, her friends, her co-workers. I let them all know that I was looking for her. I gave them all newly printed cards that had Knighthorse's office address on them.

I did this throughout the week, for hours on end, running people down as they went to work, came home from work, at lunchtime, in their offices. I harassed anyone who knew Lucy, focusing on her family, although I never did come across her sister. I also never came across the red SUV, but that was okay. I had gotten the word out—and there was no evidence that I was going to let up, either.

Now, I knew, it was just a matter of time.

My new rings worked marvelously. I could just kiss the Librarian again, and I just might. I wore one on each index finger, and with them, I was able to work most of the days while my sister watched over my kids. Additionally, I woke up easily and dreamed deeply. But best of all. Best of all...

Was the food.

Oh, God, the food...

VAMPIRE SUN

***

It had taken me two days to work up the courage to eat and in the end, I had just suggested takeout for my first meal.

"Are you nervous?" asked Kingsley on that second day. We were both staring down at a plate full of rich gnocchi from my favorite Italian restaurant—that is, back when I could have Italian food—Geno's in the City of Orange.

"A little," I said. "I mean, what if the ring doesn't work?"

"Then I expect to see you running to the bathroom. That is, if this shithole has a bathroom."

"It's outside," I said, motioning through Knighthorse's now-open pebbled-glass door. "And down the hallway."

"Classy," said Kingsley. "Well, are you going to try it or not?"

"Give me a minute."

"It's getting cold, Sam," said Kingsley, grinning. "And it looks awfully good, whatever it is. Guh-noshi."

"Gnocchi," I said, pronouncing it correctly. "And they're potatoes."

"And why again did you pick potatoes over meat for your first meal?"

"Because...they'll go down a little easier. My stomach hasn't had to digest anything other than blood in nearly a decade. Well, blood, wine and water."

"Sounds like a Christian band," said Kingsley. "Blood, Wine and Water."

"Will you just zip it?" I said. "This is serious business. You do realize that this will be the first time I will have eaten anything—"

"Yes, Sam. The first time since the last time you sneaked some Oreos a few years ago and subsequently vomited them within seconds."

"No one likes a know-it-all," I said. "And this is a momentous occasion for me."

"And you're sharing it with me," said Kingsley. "Should I be touched?"

"You should be quiet," I said, but gave him a half-smile.

He made a gesture of zipping his lips closed, locking them, and tossing away the key.

"Okay," I said. "Here goes."

Kingsley watched me with great interest and some amusement as I lifted a forkful of the still-steaming gnocchi—which Kingsley had thoughtfully brought to me on his lunch break—up from the plate and toward my lips. That it smelled heavenly went without saying. My mouth watered. A very human reaction.

"Here goes," I said.

"You said that."

"Right."

And in it went, slowly. I wrapped my lips around the fork hesitantly, cautiously, then used my teeth to scrape the gnocchi clean off. Butter, olive oil and garlic exploded in my mouth. I had wondered if my taste buds would even work. But they did—and then some. More so than I was prepared for.

"Oh, my God."

"That good, huh?"

"Mmm. Holy shit."

"Jesus, Sam. You're gonna turn me on."

But I wasn't listening to him. I was doing all I could to not dive headfirst into the greasy to-go box. Still, I waited. After all, it had only been a few seconds since that first bite. I forced myself to set aside the fork...and waited.

"What are you doing?" asked Kingsley.

"I'm waiting."

He nodded, getting it. "Oh, right. Barf city. Fingers crossed."

"Fingers and toes."

A minute went by. And then another.

"We in the clear?" asked Kingsley. "Should I run for the exit?"

"I don't know."

"Any pain?"

"No pain," I said.

"Feel like vomiting?"

"Only when I see your face."

He reached for the to-go box. "Take that back, or I'm taking back the food."

"You want another fork in your hand?"

"Sam..."

"Fine. Your face doesn't make me want to vomit. there's a small chance that you are still kind of cute. A very small chance."

"Better," he said, and retracted his hand. "I think."

A minute later, while Kingsley feasted on a boxful of riblets, I ate my second bite of gnocchi...and loved every chew. It didn't take me long to finish that box...and I was already hungry for more.

***

That had been three days ago, and I have been eating heartily ever since. Eating anything and everything. Thank the good Lord, I wasn't gaining any weight. At least, not yet.

Now, a week after canvassing the area—often with a full stomach—I finally hit pay dirt.

Pay dirt in this case was the sound of a car pulling up outside of Knighthorse's office. I pushed aside the Cinnabon I had been devouring and closed my eyes, casting my mind out, and saw her emerge from a blue compact car. Dark hair, big glasses. It was her, minus the wig. She had dyed her hair.

I licked my sticky fingers clean and shot Detective Sharp a quick text: *She's here*.

Detective Sharp knew where I was, of course, although he hadn't been too keen on the plan. Next, still using the iPhone, I swiped over to the audio app and pressed "record."

Oh, the wonders of technology.

42.

I waited patiently behind the desk.

A moment later, the door opened and a woman stepped inside. It was Lucy Gleason, and I was excited, although I didn't show it.

"Samantha Moon?" she asked.

"You got her," I said cheerfully.

"May I come in?"

"You may."

She did so, closing the door behind her. A small woman, even smaller than myself. She was cute, too, until you remembered she had hid out in a women's bathroom for five days.

She looked at me from just inside the door. I sat behind Knighthorse's leather-tooled desk. It didn't fit the ambiance of the bullet-riddled room, which was covered in pictures of Knighthorse himself, depicting him back in his college football days.

Lucy had big, round, baleful eyes, complete with half-moon shaped dark bags hanging underneath. "I assume you know who I am," she said.

"Have a seat, Lucy."

She did, picking the middle of three client chairs. I wondered when and if Knighthorse ever had three clients in here at one time. *Ever the optimist,* I suspected he would say.

"You did it," she said.

"I did."

"You flushed me out."

"I can see that."

"I had to come see you just so you would leave my family and friends alone."

"How many knew of your disappearance?"

"Only one, my sister...and one friend."

"Who drove the red SUV?"

"My sister."

"Whose red SUV is it?"

"Her co-worker's. She borrowed it for the day. Told them she was picking something up."

"Boy, did she."

"Yes," said Lucy.

Dammit, I liked her. She had a calmness to her that I admired. A tranquility that I not only craved, but seemed elusive. At least to me. But she had it, except I doubted that she'd always had it.

She has it now, I thought. *Now that she is free.*

"Why did you do it?" I asked. "Why Starbucks?

Why at that moment and time?"

She looked over at my cell phone, which wasn't doing a very good job of hiding itself behind the lamp. "I assume you're recording this."

"You assume correctly."

She nodded. I was tempted to dip into her thoughts, but her aura was bright blue, which was the color I associated with honesty. Green would have been a different story. So, I waited, knowing I was going to at least hear some semblance of truth.

"I've wanted leave Henry for some time."

"Most people do just that...leave," I said. "Most don't hide in a Starbucks's bathroom."

"I chose the location very carefully," she said.

"Not a coffee fan?"

"You would think, but no. This Starbucks is unique in that it only has one main opening, no drive-thru, nor any open windows."

I said, "And this was important to you, why?"

She shook her head. "You tell me, Samantha Moon. You've already figured out so much. Obviously, you sat through five days of tape."

"Mostly on fast forward," I said.

"And yet, you spotted me leaving."

"I have good eyes."

"Remarkable eyes," she added.

"Don't try to butter me up, missy. You're still in hot water. And why do I suddenly sound like Dick Tracy?"

She laughed lightly at that. A high, refined laugh.

I laughed, too, not so high, and not so refined, and had I known her a little better, I might have thrown in a snort.

When we were done laughing, I considered her reasons for disappearing in this particular setting. I could cheat, of course, and dip into her mind. Except I didn't feel like cheating. I did the next best thing: I puzzled it out aloud.

"For some reason, you chose a location with only one entrance and one rear exit. A location with no other obvious security cameras, except the one perched high in the parking lot."

"Keep going."

"Most important, you must have somehow come across the vent under the bathroom sink. Maybe you dropped your eyeliner—or a paper towel. You looked down and saw the vent partially open. You pulled it all the way open, and saw that, wonder of wonders, you could fit inside. At that point, you checked yourself in for some serious therapy."

"Very funny, Ms. Moon. Continue."

"Continuing. Now that you found a possible location to stage your disappearance, you would have come back and staked out the parking lot, perhaps under disguise and out of sight of the camera. Inside, you already noticed there were no cameras, which is what you would have wanted. You didn't want to be recorded entering the premises."

"Keep going, Ms. Moon. You're doing wonderfully."

VAMPIRE SUN

I tapped my fingernails on the desk. Until I remembered that my nails looked like something out of a Frankenstein movie. I retracted my hands. Ever the freak. I said, "You wanted the exterior camera to document your disappearance. To prove you went in."

"Very good."

I bit my lip, thinking hard. "But you wanted to create the illusion of truly disappearing, which is why you waited five long days, thinking that was surely long enough for any normal person to quit watching the video feeds...and to give up looking for you."

"Or so I thought," said Lucy. "Which implies that you, my good lady, may not be normal."

"You have no idea," I said, and left it at that. "Moving on. Your disappearance, then, was well documented. Your reappearance, not so much. And it took some luck on my part to even notice you. Admittedly, at that point, I was close to giving up looking."

"Your perseverance is admirable," she said.

"Again, quit trying to get on my good side."

"I'm only stating the facts, Ms. Moon. Continue, if you will. This is fun."

"Your disappearance baffled everyone, including the police and the public at large. The police opened up a missing person's case, although not a homicide case, because no body was found, and no one, really, had any clue what happened to you."

"Keep going, Sam. You're close."

I felt it, too. This time, I tapped my nails on the desk's drawer, near my leg, and out of sight of her eyes. "There were no suspects because no crime appeared to have been committed. Even your husband—and husbands are usually the first suspects—wasn't really considered a suspect. At least, not after the initial questioning and viewing of the tape. Once your disappearance had been established, your husband was no longer deemed a suspect." I shook my head. "I'm sorry, that's all I've got."

"You circled it, Samantha. You got so close. I'll fill in the blanks." She sat forward, collected herself. "I love my husband. But I'm not in love with him. My husband is also abusive."

"Physically?"

"Sometimes. But mostly, verbally and psychologically."

"Hold on," I said, and now I did scan her thoughts, her memories. There he was, yelling at her. There he was, holding her against a wall by the throat. There he was, threatening her. There he was, weeping over his poor judgment and begging her to take him back.

"Did he ever hurt you?" I asked.

"Not really; he just scared me."

"I think I understand now," I said.

"Enlighten me," she said, sitting back.

"You wanted out, but you wanted to punish him, too."

"Very good, Sam."

"You wanted him to always wonder what happened to you, to perhaps never find a moment's rest again."

"Very, very good, Sam."

"And in the process, you could start a new life somewhere. Start over. I take it you had no kids."

"None, and not a lot of family either."

"Just your sister," I said. "Who knew about the plot."

"Yes, the *plot*. I like that."

"And had you just walked away, hopped on a plane somewhere and started over..."

"My husband, more than likely, would have been arrested for murdering me. There were enough phone calls to the police to warrant that."

"You could have just divorced him."

"He threatened to come after me, to never let me go. To make my life a living hell."

"But you loved him."

"Enough to not want to see him rot in jail."

"But not enough to not traumatize him."

"I lived with similar trauma for many years. He was due. He loves me. I know that. But he is not a good man."

I looked at her and suddenly appreciated the depth of her cunning. "So, you disappeared in such a way—a documented way—that your husband wouldn't be a suspect. A true disappearance."

"Yes."

"And he would always wonder, perhaps until

the day he died, what happened to you."

A long, slow smile spread over her face. "Yes, Sam. Oh, yes."

"And you would be free to start over."

"That was the plan."

"All while your husband suffered and drove himself mad."

"It would serve him right."

I drummed my fingers on the edge of drawer. "You are a devious woman, Lucy Gleason."

"I've had many years to cook up my escape, Ms. Moon."

"I assume you have fake passports, fake identities."

"You name it," she said, "and I have it."

"So, you can truly start over somewhere."

"Yes, at least, that was the dream."

"There is, of course, the small matter of the dead homicide investigator," I said. "Detective Renaldo."

"Yes, I heard, from my sister, that he had passed. You think I had anything to do with that?"

I scanned her thoughts, scanned them deeply and completely, and saw that she hadn't. Saw, in fact, that she would never commit such a heinous act. I felt her horror at just the thought of it. His death had been a true hit and run. Maybe I would throw in a freebie for the Corona Police Department and run down Renaldo's killer. *Maybe, we'll see.*

"No," I said, finally. "I don't think that at all."

"So, what do we do now?"

"*We* don't do anything," I said. "*You*, on the other hand, would do well to disappear. I hear Borneo is nice this time of year."

"Your tape..."

"Will be erased."

"Would you mind if I watched you erase it? Sorry, but I've been on the run for a few weeks now, and I'm a little, ah, paranoid."

"*No problemo*," I said, busting out my Spanish. I showed her my phone, and then had her watch as I erased the latest audio recording, *her* audio recording.

"Thank you, Samantha Moon," she said. She reached over the desk and shook my hand, flinching only slightly at my ice-cold touch. Then she nodded, thanked me again, and left.

I watched her leave, and then waited for Detective Sharp to come all the way over from Corona, before I gave him the bad news that it had been a case of mistaken identity.

Oh, and there was also the matter of wiping his memory clean of me finding her on the tape...and anyone else in his department he might have told.

I smiled at that...

And so did the demon inside me.

43.

"Are you alone?" I asked.

I was sitting with my back against a brick wall. I held my phone loosely against my ear. I had to, because I was dripping sweat. I had gone for a long jog, and had done a lot of hard thinking while I ran.

My jog had led me to here, many miles from my home.

"I've been alone for a long time now, Sam," said the deep voice on the other end. A voice that was deeper than most men, which made sense, since his lung capacity was much bigger, too. Much bigger by a lot.

"You mean from the parade of young, nubile women coming and going in and out of your house at all hours of the night and day?"

"Jesus, Sam. It was never like that. Well, maybe for a few years, but never like what you just described."

"A full decade is more than a few years."

"Not when you're something like me," said Kingsley, who always hated talking about who we really were on the phone.

"And me," I said.

"Two freaks," he said.

"That's my line," I said, and watched a moth flutter around the outdoor light. Now, two moths. They looked a tad confused. I wondered if they thought they were circling the sun.

"I miss you, Sam," he said, and I heard his voice break. "I've missed you ever since my stupid mistake."

"Stupid, stupid mistake," I said.

"I've missed you every day, of every hour, and I have been empty ever since."

"You've dated..."

"I've *tried* to date. Nothing's worked out. Truth was, I didn't want anything to work out. I wanted you back. I want you back now."

"Why?"

"Because you're my girl, Samantha Moon."

"Am I now?"

"Yes. I felt it from the moment I first laid eyes on you."

"The moment you first laid eyes on me, I was a married woman."

"And I was respectful," he said. "I waited. And

when we did start dating, I knew you weren't in a good place. I sensed you were skittish, hurt, and not ready for anything too deep or too fast. I kept my distance, and let you find your way to me. And then, you did. And I was so happy."

I didn't say anything. I didn't have to. We both knew what had happened next.

And, for the first time, I let his mistake go...and I forgave him. Maybe not completely, but enough to move on.

"So, what do we do now?" I asked.

And for an answer, the front door swung open, and Kingsley stared down at me from high above, his shaggy hair almost covering his face entirely. He was still holding his phone to his ear.

"Stay with me," he said. "Tonight. One night is all I ask."

He reached down, and I looked long and hard at his thick paw...then took his hand. He lifted me to my feet effortlessly...and pulled me into his arms. I went willingly enough.

"One night," I said, lifting my face.

"One night is all I need," he said, lowering his face to mine, and he kissed me harder than he'd ever kissed me before.

And he kissed me like that all night long...and well into morning.

The End

About the Author:

J.R. Rain is an ex-private investigator who now writes full-time. He lives in a small house on a small island with his small dog, Sadie. Please visit him at www.jrrain.com.

BW Mar/18

62231849R00130

Made in the USA
Middletown, DE
19 January 2018